Elbridge S. Brooks

The Century Book of Famous Americans

the story of a young people's pilgrimage to historic homes

Elbridge S. Brooks

The Century Book of Famous Americans
the story of a young people's pilgrimage to historic homes

ISBN/EAN: 9783337299545

Printed in Europe, USA, Canada, Australia, Japan

Cover: Foto ©Andreas Hilbeck / pixelio.de

More available books at **www.hansebooks.com**

STATUE OF ABRAHAM LINCOLN.

ISSUED UNDER THE AUSPICES OF THE NATIONAL SOCIETY
OF THE DAUGHTERS OF THE AMERICAN REVOLUTION

THE CENTURY BOOK
OF FAMOUS AMERICANS

THE STORY OF A YOUNG PEOPLE'S
PILGRIMAGE TO HISTORIC HOMES

BY

ELBRIDGE S. BROOKS

AUTHOR OF "THE CENTURY BOOK FOR YOUNG AMERICANS,"
"HISTORIC BOYS," "A BOY OF THE FIRST EMPIRE," ETC.

WITH PORTRAITS AND MANY OTHER ILLUSTRATIONS

THE CENTURY CO., NEW YORK

THE DE VINNE PRESS.

INTRODUCTION

OFFICE OF THE PRESIDENT-GENERAL, NATIONAL SOCIETY
OF THE DAUGHTERS OF THE AMERICAN REVOLUTION.

WASHINGTON, D. C., June 18, 1896.

THE organization of the National Society of the Daughters of the American Revolution was the outgrowth of that notable epoch in American history when from the Pacific coast the tidal wave of patriotic enthusiasm started, and by its might and power kindled in the hearts of men and women interest in the Colonial and Revolutionary periods which had so long lain dormant.

The National Society of the Daughters of the American Revolution was organized in Washington, D. C., October 11, 1890. Its objects are: "(1) To perpetuate the memory and the spirit of the men and women who achieved American Independence, by the acquisition and protection of historic spots and the erection of monuments; by the encouragement of historical research in relation to the Revolution, and the publication of its results; by the preservation of documents and relics, and of the records of the individual services of Revolutionary soldiers and patriots, and by the promotion of celebrations of all patriotic anniversaries. (2) To carry out the injunction of Washington in his farewell address to the American people: 'To promote, as an object of primary importance, institutions for the general diffusion of knowledge,' thus developing an enlightened public opinion, and affording to young and old such advantages as shall develop in them the largest capacity for performing the duties of American citizens. (3) To cherish, maintain, and extend the institutions of American freedom, to foster true patriotism and love of country, and to aid in securing for mankind all the blessings of liberty."

To-day the National Society of the Daughters of the American Revolution, numbering fourteen thousand five hundred, supplemented by the organization of the National Society of the Children of the American Revolution, numbering fourteen hundred and thirty, whose motto is, "For God and country," stand united, to maintain the objects of the National Society as presented in the constitution and by-laws of the Daughters of the American Revolution.

By the authority of the National Board of Managers this brief introduction is written, and it is a free-will offering. It may be well, further, to state that the National Society of the Daughters of the American Revolution have no other interest in "The Century Book of Famous Americans" than to wish it all success in its endeavor to place before the youth of our country an account of the lives of some of the men who have helped to make America famous.

LETITIA GREEN STEVENSON,
President-General.

THE GARDEN AT MOUNT VERNON.

SOME BOSTON SPIRES. FROM A PRINT (1758) IN THE KING'S COLLECTION IN THE BRITISH MUSEUM.

TABLE OF CONTENTS

THE CENTURY BOOK
OF FAMOUS AMERICANS.

MOUNT VERNON IN 1796.

THE CENTURY BOOK
OF FAMOUS AMERICANS

CHAPTER I

IN BOSTON TOWN

The Birthplace of Franklin — The Story of James Otis — Tories and Traitors — The Webster Buildings — The Samuel Adams Tablet — The Father of the Revolution — A Novel Pilgrimage.

HEY had left the Old South Meeting-house with its revolutionary relics, and were slowly sauntering down the sunny side of Milk street when Jack seized his uncle's arm.

"Look over there, Uncle Tom!" he cried. "See what it says on that building: 'The Birthplace of Franklin.' Why, I did n't know that Franklin was born in Boston. I thought he was a Philadelphian."

"He was an American, Jack," Uncle Tom replied. "I sometimes think he was the first real American. But he was Boston born and bred. You ask Roger. I imagine every boy who goes to the Boston Latin School and tries for the Franklin medal knows of the clause in Franklin's will that tells the story. 'I was born in Boston,' it says. 'I owe my first instruction in literature to the free grammar schools established there.' And so he set aside five hundred dollars, the interest from which was to provide, forever, for silver medals for 'the most deserving boys' of what afterward became the English High and Latin schools of his native town. But, though born in Boston, Philadelphia was the home of Franklin for the greater part of his life."

"Why, yes; of course I know that, Uncle Tom," Marian declared. "Don't you remember the story, Jack, about Franklin's first day in Philadelphia?"

1

"To be sure I do," broke in Jack; "that's when he saw the girl who afterward became his wife, with a loaf of bread under each arm, eating another."

Marian laughed so merrily at this that people in the street turned to see who could be so very hilarious in the shadow of the Old South.

"Now, is n't that just like Jack?" she cried. "You'd think it was Franklin's wife who was eating the bread. And how could any one walk the streets with a loaf under each arm and eating another? Franklin did n't have three hands, did he?"

"I guess I put a loaf too many in the story," Jack confessed. "But what of that? Franklin could have eaten it that way if any one could. He was smart enough to do anything. And so that 's where he was born, is it?"

"That 's the spot," said Uncle Tom. Some people declare his birthplace was down on Hanover street, but it now seems pretty certain that the little Milk street house was the right one."

"But not in that tailor's shop, surely," said Christine. "Why, it does n't look nearly old enough."

"Of course not," Marian decided. "Why, Franklin was born in —— when was he born, Uncle Tom?"

"Seventeenth of January, 1706," promptly replied her uncle, who, as all the boys and girls declared, was always "great on dates."

"I 'm afraid," he continued, "your making the birthplace of Franklin out of that iron building across the way about equals Jack's three arms, though I must say that the stories all uphold Jack's three loaves."

"Aha! Miss Smarty; what did I tell you?" cried Jack, trium-

THE OLD SOUTH CHURCH, BOSTON.
Franklin's birthplace is opposite the further end.

phantly. "I said Franklin could do it. I 'm going to try it some day."

"No; that building over there is, of course, on the site of Franklin's birthplace," Uncle Tom explained. "It simply marks with its memorial tablet the spot on which stood, until the year 1810, the queer little top-heavy wooden cottage in which Benjamin Franklin was born."

"That was a good deal like Franklin himself, was n't it, Uncle Tom?" Bert commented — "heavy in the upper story, you know."

"Good enough, Bert!" laughed Uncle Tom. "Yes; you may say it was typical. I wish we had more such tablets as that one over the way. It is one of the best history teachers for young Americans that I know of — and for old ones, too," he added. "But come; let 's move on. There 's nothing else about that building to remind us of Franklin, and Faneuil Hall is n't far away."

FRANKLIN'S BIRTHPLACE.
House formerly on Milk street, Boston.

They had arrived in Boston that morning on a sight-seeing tour — Uncle Tom Dunlap and his nephews Jack Dunlap and Albert Upham, his niece Marian Dunlap, and her "best friend" Christine Bacon. Of course you remember them — that group of wide-awake boys and girls who, under Uncle Tom's guidance, "did" Washington so thoroughly, from the Constitution to the Capitol, and studied into the making of the American nation.

In the dark doorway of Faneuil Hall Roger was waiting, according to appointment, to welcome and join them. You remember him too, I hope — Roger Densmore, "the boy from Boston." He was to do the honors of "the Hub" for the young folks from "Gotham."

They inspected Faneuil Hall with due reverence.

"Who called it the Cradle of Liberty, Uncle Tom?" Christine inquired, as they descended the stairs and walked across to Quincy Market.

"James Otis, another famous Bostonian," Uncle Tom replied. "He delivered the address of dedication when this hall was rebuilt. He was the man who really started the American Revolution, you know."

"What! James Otis?" cried Jack. "Why, I thought Patrick Henry

Drawn from the Original
Jan. 11th 1866 -

A BOSTON BOY WHO BECAME FAMOUS.

Benjamin Franklin. Born in Boston in 1706.

did that — the 'gentlemen-may-cry-peace-peace-but-there-is-no-peace' man."

"No; historians give the credit largely to Otis," Uncle Tom replied. " He really made the first move toward independence, years before Patrick Henry's fiery speech. For when, in 1761, four years before the passage of the Stamp Act, James Otis, in the Superior Court of Massachusetts, in this very town of Boston, resisted the granting of what were called the Writs of Assistance, the first scene of the first act of opposition to British tyranny was opened. 'Then and there,' declared John Adams, fifty years after, ' the child Independence was born.' So, let us give to James Otis the credit that is justly due him."

"All right; let him have it ! " said Jack, administering an appreciative and emphatic slap to a particularly large beef carcass that hung obtrusively in his path.

"Whereabouts did he live, Uncle Tom?" asked Bert.

" Right here in Boston, Bert," his uncle replied.

"Oh, can't we see the house ? " Marian inquired. " Somehow, it always makes people seem more real if one can only see where they once lived; does n't it, Christine? "

"I don't believe his house is standing now," said Uncle Tom. " Do you know, Roger?"

Roger was obliged to confess his ignorance, though he

THE BIRTHPLACE OF INDEPENDENCE.
Interior view of Old State House, Boston, where James Otis delivered his famous speech; chair of Elbridge Gerry; bust of James Otis.

said he believed there was something to do with Otis in the Old State House on Washington street.

"That 's where he made the famous speech, of which I told you, against the Writs of Assistance," said Uncle Tom. " We 'll go in there later. And I 'll see if I can find out about the house of James Otis. His was a brief but brilliant career, boys and girls; as sad in its ending as it was promising at the opening. He was a bright young Boston lawyer. Engaged by the British government to look after its cases in the Boston courts, he threw up his position and all its advantages, because he would not argue a case that seemed to threaten the liberties of the people. He became the people's champion, an eloquent and impassioned orator, a tireless worker for liberty, one of the leaders of the early Boston patriots, a member of the first Continental Congress, and destined, apparently, to play an important part in the drama of Independence. Then, suddenly, all changed. In a coffee-house here in Boston he was set upon by a gang of ruffianly Tories, knocked senseless, made an incurable lunatic, and, the very year that the Revolution he had started ended in success, he was killed by a stroke of lightning."

"George! that was rough, though, was n't it?" said Jack.

"Those horrid Tories!" exclaimed Marian. "Oh — I just despise them!"

"But those were rough, hard days, Marian," said Uncle Tom; "and both sides had their evil instruments. The fact that men were Tories did not make them bad. Every one has a right to his opinion; it is the way he handles his opinion that makes him either a public friend or a public foe. America has yet to learn and acknowledge the real service that the forces of opposition have done for her development."

"Oh, Uncle Tom, how can that be?" demanded Bert.

"Do you mean to say that the Tories were a benefit?" cried Marian.

"In what we call the broad sense, most certainly I do," Uncle Tom replied, "much as it inflames your ardent Americanism to hear me proclaim it. The Tories of the Revolution and the Copperheads of the Civil War, though detested by patriots, were themselves, as a rule, conscientious, honest, and kind-hearted people, who loved their homes and their families just as dearly as do your fathers and mothers. They meant well; they even loved their native land: but their standards were not as lofty, nor was their love of country as unselfish as with those whom they opposed."

"Why, Uncle Tom!" exclaimed Marian, to whom such a doctrine seemed all wrong.

"So, as I say," went on Uncle Tom, "they were really a benefit to the nation. The intense hatred they aroused in their opponents only drew the determined people closer together, and led them to stand shoulder to shoulder in defense of the cause of liberty. Even those roughs who spoiled the life of James Otis, when they struck down one patriot, inspired a dozen others to be still more ardent in the cause he championed, and to carry forward his work. Think of that, boys and girls, as you study the crises in American history. Tories and traitors, instead of weakening our cause, helped it by the spirit and will that they aroused; and these led straight to victory. That thought will help you, perhaps, better to understand Thomson's perplexing line:

"From seeming evil still educing good."

"Why, was it Thomson who said that?" queried Christine. "I thought it was Pope."

"No, my dear; it was Thomson," Uncle Tom replied. "But Pope wrote certain lines that are even more applicable to all knotty problems of whys and wherefores. Who knows them?"

No one knew just to what lines of Pope Uncle Tom referred; so,

IN TORY TIMES.
A patriot woman escaping from the Tories and the British.

as they paused before the historic wharf where the disguised patriots flung over the offending chests of tea, he repeated the lines he had in mind:

"All Nature is but Art, unknown to thee;
All Chance, Direction which thou canst not see;
All Discord, Harmony not understood;
All partial Evil, universal Good;
And, spite of Pride, in erring Reason's spite,
One truth is clear: Whatever is, is right!"

As they passed along Summer street on their way from the old wharf of the Tea Party to the enlarged and renovated State House on Beacon Hill, Uncle Tom stopped short and pointed across the way to a six-story business block at the corner of High and Summer streets.

THE STATUE OF BENJAMIN FRANKLIN.
In front of the Boston City Hall.

"See anything peculiar about that building?" he asked.
The boys and girls studied it from top to bottom.
"'The Webster Buildings,'" read Marian, looking toward the roof; while Bert's eye, traveling faster, stopped at the lettering above the second story.

"'The Home of Daniel Webster,'" he read. "Is that so? Did Daniel Webster live there?" he asked.

"I never noticed that," confessed Roger, "and I 've passed here hundreds of times."

"Roger, my boy," said Uncle Tom, "you 're not the only American who has no eyes for his own historic surroundings. Yes; the city house in which Webster lived once stood on that spot. Then, as now, it was a rounded corner; but to-day, you see, it is the heart of a business center. There he entertained Lafayette in 1824, and there he lived at the height of his fame."

"He was a great man, too, was n't he, Uncle Tom?" said Marian.

"Great in many ways," her uncle replied. "Come now, what do you know about Daniel Webster, boys and girls?"

"A great lawyer," suggested Bert.

"A great statesman," said Marian.

"A great debater," hazarded Roger.

"A great fisherman," put in Jack.

"A great American," said Christine.

"He was all of those," Uncle Tom nodded.

"He was twice Secretary of State," said Roger.

"But never President," commented Jack.

"He made a famous speech against Hayne," said Bert.

"But went back on the people who elected him," asserted Jack.

"No; did he, Uncle Tom?" demanded Marian.

"Why, yes; don't you know, that 's what Whittier's poem 'Ichabod' was all about," Christine announced. "Our history teacher told us that."

"Say, rather," said Uncle Tom, with a smile at the criticisms of his youthful convoy, "that the people progressed faster than their leader. Daniel Webster was a great man, a wise man, a noble man; but the one great question of his day, slavery, was dividing the country North and South. And when a man, however ardently he loves peace and union, tries to please two people at once, he has a hard time of it, and ends by pleasing neither. That was Daniel Webster's case; and Whittier's fiery verses, to which Christine refers, were but the expression of the advancing thought of the people of the North — too deeply roused to be calm, too strong of purpose to be discriminating. They had forged far ahead of Webster, though he had been the idol and champion of the very people who now called him recreant."

"But if he thought he was doing right," said Jack, "I call it pretty hard lines to be pitched into like that."

"My dear Jack," replied Uncle Tom, "if you are ever a leader, look ahead. Lead on to the end. Those who follow often push to the front, and the leader who lags behind is like the fellow who loses his rank in school or ' goes down foot ' — he simply ' is n't in it,' as you boys say."

They crossed Washington street and in Indian file threaded the narrow and crowded sidewalk that borders the upper side of Winter street.

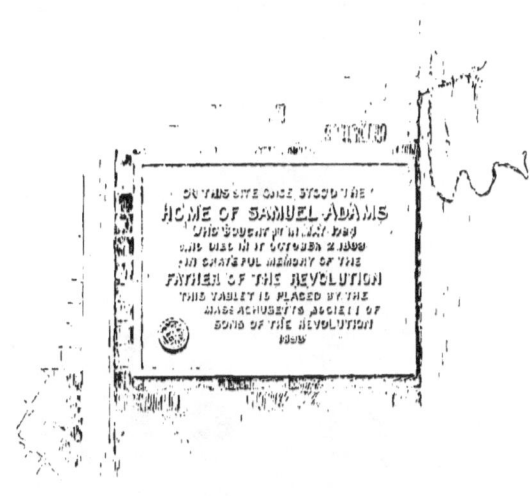

THE SITE OF THE HOME OF SAMUEL ADAMS.
On Winter Place, Boston.

At a "cañon," as Jack called it, which cleft the blocks of tall stores on Winter street and which, they saw, was called Winter Place, Uncle Tom halted his five followers, and bade them read the bronze tablet set in the dead wall of a great dry-goods store.

They did so. The tablet advised them that, on this corner, once stood the house in which lived Samuel Adams, "the Father of the Revolution."

" How many ' fathers ' did the Revolution have, anyway ?" demanded Jack.

" I thought you told us, Uncle Tom, that James Otis was its ' respected parient.' "

" I merely quoted John Adams's words to the effect that Otis was the ' father of Independence,' " Uncle Tom explained; " and, in this land of ours, the desire for independence was the forerunner of revolution."

" Then Otis was a sort of grandfather to it, was n't he ? " Jack commented.

" Samuel Adams ! " said Christine, still reading the tablet on the wall. " Did n't we see his statue somewhere down near Faneuil Hall ? "

" Yes, in Dock Square, now known as Adams Square," replied Roger.

" I thought so. ' A statesman incorruptible and fearless.' That was what it called him on the statue," said Christine.

" That was the man," Uncle Tom assented. " And that was the truth. Here he lived, and in a green plot beyond us, just below the head of Winter street, — the Old Granary Burying-Ground it is called, — he lies buried."

" Close to his old home," remarked Christine; " and we can see both places. Is n't it interesting ? "

"What relation was he to John Adams, Uncle Tom?" Bert inquired. "A brother?"

"No; John Adams was his second cousin, I believe," Uncle Tom replied. "This Samuel Adams was a great man, boys and girls, though without the calmness, the coolness, or the judgment of his greater cousin. Historians tell us that Samuel Adams was the architect of ruin, and John Adams the organizer of law."

"That means, I suppose," said Roger, "that Samuel just tore things down and John built things up, doesn't it?"

"That's about it," Uncle Tom answered. "But an old building must be pulled down before you can build a grand new one in its place. Samuel

OLD DOCK SQUARE (NOW ADAMS SQUARE).
A famous old Boston site. Faneuil Hall in the distance, the Adams statue in the foreground.

Adams was a rebel against the English crown from boyhood, although his father was a tax-collector for the government, and Adams himself filled such a position for a time. When he graduated from Harvard in 1740, his commencement oration was a plea for resistance to tyranny. He held to that belief all through life. He was the leader and chosen representative of the people—'the tribune of the yeomanry,' some one has called him. He urged on the 'embattled farmers' of Lexington and Concord to fire

THE GRAVE OF SAMUEL ADAMS.
In the southern end of Old Granary Burying-Ground.

'the shot heard round the world,' of which you possibly know something — "

"Emerson wrote that," said Roger in earnest undertone.

"Tell me something new, Roger, my son," said Jack. "Do you think we never went to school?"

"Samuel Adams was fearless, sincere, unyielding, and absolutely incorruptible," Uncle Tom continued. "He proposed the Revolution; he proposed the Continental Congress; he signed the Declaration of Independence, and was so sharp a thorn in the side of the British government and its generals that they tried first to bribe and then to kill him. But they could neither bribe nor kill him. He lived to see the troops of King George driven from Boston and finally from America, and the principles for which he labored and suffered everywhere triumphant. Free America owes much to Samuel Adams. On this very corner stood his home. Uncover to it, boys, for it was the home of a patriot."

The enthusiastic five honored the prosaic dead wall with a Chautauqua salute, much to the astonishment of the passers-by, few of whom, probably, ever knew of the existence of the tablet or the historic associations of that busy corner. Familiarity rarely inspires investigation.

They "did" the old town thoroughly during their week's visit. They inspected its "show places," from Copp's Hill to Dorchester Heights, and from Cambridge Common to Bunker Hill. They studied the old grave-yards, eloquent with the names of famous ones dead and gone; they went back into the past as far as the one remaining wall of the Old Province House which Hawthorne has immortalized, and forward in the present to the, splendid new Public Library and the unfinished Subway that burrows beneath the Autocrat's dear " Long Walk."

But Uncle Tom discovered that the homes of famous men, or the spots upon which such houses had stood, seemed to possess special interest.

THE MAIN STAIRCASE IN THE BOSTON PUBLIC LIBRARY.

One of Louis St. Gaudens's "lions," in commemoration of the Massachusetts troops.

"It brings you so near to them," Christine declared; and even the intensely modern and practical Jack affirmed that it was as great fun "hunting up the stamping-grounds of all those old Boston fellows" as shooting up to the twelfth story of the Ames Building, or seeing a ball game on Soldiers' Field — and you may be sure that Jack did both these things.

PARK STREET GATE, BOSTON COMMON.
The State House in the distance.

Under Roger's guidance, and with Uncle Tom as showman, they visited the sites of Franklin's boyhood home and John Hancock's vanished mansion; they found the place in Court street where the house of James Otis had stood; they looked up the sites of Warren's, Everett's, Sumner's, Wendell Phillips's, and Prescott's homes; of the birthplaces of Paul Revere, who roused the country-side for Lexington fight, and of Morse, who invented the telegraph — the plain wooden house almost in the shadow of Bunker Hill.

"And all these are in Boston!" exclaimed Bert.

"Good for the Hub!" cried Jack. "Is there any other town that can show so many, Uncle Tom?"

Whereupon Uncle Tom had an idea.

"He 's full of 'em," Jack declared; "but this just tops them all."

It did seem to. For it was nothing more or less than a pilgrimage to the homes of famous Americans.

A BOSTON HOME IN GREAT-GREAT-GRANDFATHER'S DAY.

"I think we can do it leisurely and as we have the chance," said Uncle Tom; "and I don't believe your fathers and mothers will object. We 'll see about it, anyhow. So, while we are here, we may as well finish off Massachusetts by hunting up the homes of John Adams at Quincy, and of Daniel

Webster at Marshfield. I'd like to see them myself. We can do it easily. What do you say, boys and girls?"

What could they say but "Good for you, Uncle Tom"?

They said it so emphatically and delightedly that Uncle Tom believed his idea to be both wise and practical, and the fifth day of their stay in Boston saw them all at the Old Colony depot, en route for Quincy, the old town made famous by the two Adamses — father and son.

A DISTANT GLIMPSE OF BOSTON.
As seen across country from the Arnold Arboretum.

CHAPTER II

Quincy Granite and Quincy Men — The Little Old Houses — "Sink or Swim" — On Penn's Hill — A Great Father and His Famous Son — An Historic Mansion.

HROUGH the lengthening line of suburban towns, now beside blue water, now in sight of the misty Milton hills, the tourists rode for a brief half hour; then, above the trees, they caught the glitter of a graceful dome, and Uncle Tom told them they were in Quincy.

"Famous alike for its granite and for its men," he said, as he helped the girls to the station platform, and together they walked up the street to the open square before the temple-like church with its gilded dome.

"Out of those quarries on the hills yonder," he continued, "has come the gray rock that has gone into many a noble public building; and from this old town have come men who have built themselves into the history of the nation. And I think, boys and girls," he added, "that we shall find the Quincy men even more enduring than the Quincy granite. Especially the Adamses."

"Did they all come from here?" inquired Roger.

"Those did whom we know best," replied Uncle Tom.

"I thought you said Sam Adams was a Boston boy," remarked Bert.

"So he was," his uncle answered. "But his 'forebears,' as they call them, came from here; for the Quincy of to-day was all Braintree in Old Colony days. The John Adams branch of the family, however, is especially remarkable. Just think! It gave to the republic two Presidents, a Vice-President, a Secretary of State, one senator, three members of Congress, and three ministers to England."

"That's a good record for one family," declared Bert.

"Anything left for anybody else?" queried Jack.

"I ought to explain, however," continued Uncle Tom, "that these dozen offices represent really but three persons — father, son, and grandson — in this celebrated family."

THE JOHN ADAMS AND THE JOHN QUINCY ADAMS HOUSES, QUINCY.

"But that makes it all the more remarkable, Uncle Tom," Christine declared.

"Besides these three," went on Uncle Tom, "the Adamses of Quincy have contributed soldiers, lawyers, legislators, educators, and writers, all of whom have done splendid work for America. It is a remarkable record, indeed."

"Who were the three special Adamses, Uncle Tom?" queried Marian. "John Adams, of course —"

"John Adams, — the 'first Adams,' he is called, though eight generations preceded him here, — John Quincy Adams, his son, and Charles Francis Adams, *his* son," Uncle Tom replied. "I call this illustrious three an inheritance by talent. Think of it! John Adams, the father, was President of the United States, and had been minister to England at the close of the American Revolution; John Quincy Adams, the son, was President

JOHN ADAMS.

Second President of the United States.

of the United States, and had been minister to England during the War of 1812; Charles Francis Adams, the grandson, just missed nomination for President of the United States, and had been minister to England during the Great Rebellion of 1861. Is n't that an honorable record for three generations? Come! there 's our car. You have seen the spot in Boston upon which stood the home of 'Cousin Sam Adams'; now we can look upon the real houses in which were born and bred these famous Adamses of Quincy."

Thereupon they all boarded the Braintree "electric," and were soon skimming along Franklin street to where, a mile beyond, at the foot of Penn's Hill, stand what are known as the "Adams houses."

"Nothing very grand or imposing about either of those old houses," was Bert's critical comment.

"Little and shabby, eh?" remarked Roger.

IN PRESIDENT JOHN ADAMS'S DAY.
A taste of war with France — the "Boston" raking "Le Berceau."

"I should say so!" exclaimed out-spoken Jack. "Why, I supposed the Adamses were very high and mighty people with big estates and grand houses."

"Far from it," said Uncle Tom. "John Adams's father, who built the old house on our left, was a thrifty Braintree farmer, worth about seven or eight thousand dollars in lands and goods. But he managed to send his son to Harvard, from which the boy graduated in 1755, and from there went to teaching school in Worcester. John Adams was born in 1735, in the right-hand front room in that little old house; John Quincy Adams was born in

HOW JOHN ADAMS HELPED MAKE THE FOURTH OF JULY.
Reporting the Declaration of Independence.

1767, in the red house on the right. I don't know that, in all the world, I can show you another scene like this—the birthplaces of two Presidents elbowing each other, and standing all these years unhonored. Now, I believe, the design is to place both these historic houses in charge of societies for their preservation."

The children stood silent awhile regarding these two unpretentious houses, from which came two men so famous in American history—and these two father and son! Then Marian exclaimed:

"Oh, Uncle Tom! Was n't it John Adams who was the 'sink-or-swim' man?"

"There never was any such man," declared Bert. "Our history teacher told us that was just a 'fake' speech."

"Did he say 'fake,' Bert?" queried Roger.

Uncle Tom was a bit puzzled at this irruption; but he was accustomed to the unconventional speech of his earnest young people, and it speedily dawned upon him what the 'sink-or-swim man' meant.

"Ah, I see!" he said; "You mean that supposed speech put into the mouth of John Adams by Daniel Webster in his famous eulogy on Adams and Jefferson — 'Sink or swim—'"

"Oh, I know that!" broke in Jack, who was not to be repressed when such an opportunity offered. " 'Sink or swim, live or die, survive or perish, I give my hand and my heart to this vote.' Say, that was not a fake speech, though, really, was it. Uncle Tom? It is too good not to be true."

"If by 'fake,'" laughed Uncle Tom, "you boys mean rigged up to suit the occasion, I 'm afraid it was. If my memory is correct, however, Webster had authority for introducing the words into his splendid eulogy. John Adams never did make just such a speech; but he did say, in a letter to his friend Sewall, in 1774, when the colonies were feeling their way toward independence, that the die was cast and he had 'passed the Rubicon.' Then he added, 'sink or swim, survive or perish with my country, is my unalterable determination.'"

"Give that to your history teacher, Master Bert, when you see him again," cried Jack. "Daniel Webster knew what he was about. But, anyhow, Uncle Tom, John Adams was the original fire-cracker man, was n't he?"

"Your descriptive adjectives, boys and girls, are certainly expressive, even if they are a trifle baffling," Uncle Tom rejoined, laughing. "Yes; John Adams was, I suppose, the father of the Fourth of July—or, at least, its prophet. Only, with him, it happened to be the second of July. That was the day — not the Fourth — on which the Congress passed Richard Henry Lee's famous resolution, which declared the United Colonies to be ' free and independent States.' That was the day of which John Adams, in writing home to his patriotic wife, here in Quincy, made his famous prophecy."

"What was it?" inquired Christine.

"As nearly as I can recall it," said Uncle Tom, "John Adams wrote: ' This second of July, 1776, will be the most memorable epoch in the history of America. I am apt to believe that it will be celebrated by succeeding generations as the great Anniversary Festival. It ought to be commemorated as the day of deliverance by solemn acts of devotion to Almighty God. It ought to be solemnized with pomp and parade, with shows, games, sports, guns, bells, bonfires, and illuminations from one end of the continent to the other from this time forward, forevermore!'"

As the children applauded the sentiment, Uncle Tom added slyly, "nothing about fire-crackers in all that, Jack."

But Jack replied: "Well, all the rest of it has come true. I guess we can squeeze in the fire-crackers between the guns and the bells, can't we?" And he gave a nod of satisfaction as the memories of all his Fourth of July fun in summers past flashed through his mind.

RINGING IN THE FOURTH.

They had left the "birthplace houses" behind and were climbing Penn's Hill, from which little eight-year old John Quincy Adams and his mother watched the smoke of Bunker Hill fight, on a certain famous seventeenth of June, and a year later watched the British fleeing from Boston.

Then Uncle Tom said:

"That mother was a remarkable woman, too. You girls must some day get acquainted with Abigail Adams, the clever wife of John. But let me tell you, boys, John Adams was something of a prophet. When he was but a young fellow, the French and Indian war was being fought in America. Its purpose was, you know, to drive the French from Canada and make this continent English. That was the war that brought George Washington to the front. Well, in the very year of Braddock's defeat young John Adams declared that, if the English soldiers and colonists could only succeed in driving out the French, the colonists would increase until, in another century, they would exceed the British, and then, 'all England will be unable to subdue us.' A good, clear-sighted bit of prophecy for a young college graduate, was n't it?"

"He 's not the only Harvard man that has had brains," said Roger.

"Hear the boy!" cried Jack. "I guess Yale has had quite as many."

"Yes, and Columbia, too," said Bert. "But, there! that 's the trouble with you Boston fellows. You just think Harvard —"

ABIGAIL ADAMS.
Mrs. John Adams at the age of 22.

"Here, here!" cried Uncle Tom, "we are not in Quincy to fight over college supremacy. When it comes to making men and patriots, no school or college has the monopoly. Of the twenty-three Presidents of the United States fifteen were college graduates; but among the remaining eight are the names of Washington and Lincoln—so, I think, we'll leave the college standard out of the reckoning. For, after all, boys and girls, success depends upon the man. Immortality comes because of deeds, not diplomas."

"But surely, Uncle Tom," said Christine, "education is necessary."

"Think how much better even Washington and Lincoln might have been if they had been college men," said Bert.

"'T is education forms the common mind:
Just as the twig is bent the tree 's inclined,"

quoted Roger, who knew his "Moral Essays."

A DINNER PARTY IN JOHN QUINCY ADAMS'S DAY.

"But there you 're out, Roger, my boy," cried Jack. "Washington and Lincoln were not 'common minds.'"

"Oh, well! the exception proves the rule," was Roger's comment.

"I think Roger has the best of the argument, after all," laughed Uncle Tom; "especially when we remember that Washington founded a university and that Lincoln was forever studying. And, speaking of Lincoln, do you know that his greatest act was based upon a doctrine first propounded by John Quincy Adams — the man who was born in that old farmhouse yonder?"

"His greatest act! What do you mean, Uncle Tom?" queried Bert. "The Emancipation Proclamation?"

"That 's it," his uncle replied. "It was upon a declaration made in Congress by John Quincy Adams in 1836 that Abraham Lincoln rested his great proclamation."

"What was it?" asked Marian.

"It was in the course of a speech that Adams pronounced this opinion: 'From the instant that your slave-holding States become the theater of war,—

civil, servile, or foreign.— from that instant the war powers of the Constitution extend to interference with the institution of slavery in every way in which it can be interfered with.' And, in a later speech, he repeated this

JOHN QUINCY ADAMS.
Sixth President of the United States.

bold doctrine, and declared that, in the event of such a war, the President of the United States had power to order the universal emancipation of the slaves."

" Why, did they say much about slavery in Adams's day?" inquired Christine. " I thought all that came later."

" Most certainly they did, my dear," Uncle Tom replied. " John Quincy Adams was the earliest and stoutest champion of antislavery in the American Congress. In fact, it was his burning words in behalf of freedom, and what was called 'the right of petition,' that gave him his popular title of 'the Old Man Eloquent.'"

"And was he so old?" Christine asked.

"At that time, yes," Uncle Tom answered. "John Quincy Adams, you know, was elected to Congress long after he had served as President. His was the only instance in our history of an ex-President of the republic serving in Congress; and he gained a new and enduring reputation by his courage and ability there. Don't you remember, when we were in Washington, that we saw the place in the Capitol where John Quincy Adams was stricken down with paralysis while in his seat in the House of Representatives? He was then over eighty years old, and, as you see, he literally 'died in harness.'"

SILHOUETTE OF JOHN Q. ADAMS.
Cut in the White House.

"I thought he died on the Fourth of July," said Jack.

"That only shows how apt we are to mix up this remarkable father and son," Uncle Tom declared. "It was John Adams — 'grandsire John,' as they called him here in Quincy — who died on the fiftieth anniversary of the Declaration of Independence — that mighty paper, which he was so largely instrumental in having adopted that men called him the 'Colossus of Independence.' And on that same Fourth of July, 1826, died also Thomas Jefferson, his political rival and successor in the Presidency, the real author of the great Declaration."

"Well, do please set them straight for us, Uncle Tom," Marian requested. "I know they were both Presidents, and that John Quincy Adams was John Adams's son. But just what did they do?"

"That should be easy to set right," Uncle Tom said. And as they turned once more from the by-path that led from Penn's Hill into Franklin street, Uncle Tom sketched the careers of the two Adamses while the party walked leisurely back to the center of the town.

"John Adams," he said, "was born in that little gray house to the left in the year 1735. His son, John Quincy Adams was born in 1767, in the old red house to the right. John Adams was elected President by the Federalists in 1796. John Quincy Adams was made President in 1824 by the 'coalition' which, later, became first the Whigs, and then the Republicans. John Adams died in the old mansion I shall soon show you at the other

end of town, on the Fourth of July, 1826; John Quincy Adams died in
the Capitol at Washington, on the 23d of February, 1848. John Adams was
bold, outspoken, upright, and true.   He always had what is called the courage of his convictions; but he was sometimes conceited, long-winded, and
brusque.   He was a great reader, a vigorous writer, and always a patriot.
The acts of his life that most entitle him to fame were his defense of the
British soldiers, unwisely tried for murder, after the so-called 'Boston massacre' of 1770; — "

"That's what that 'slate-pencil' monument on Boston Common is for,
you know," whispered Roger to Jack.

" — the proposing of Washington as commander-in-chief of the American Army in 1775," went on Uncle Tom; "the speech on the first of July,
1776, which resulted in the adoption of the Declaration of Independence;
the recognition by Holland of the new nation of the United States of America, and the Dutch loan, which put money in the pocket of the young re-

THE PUBLIC LIBRARY, QUINCY, MASS.

public — both of these being secured by him in 1782; the great treaty with
England, which he 'achieved' in 1783; his patriotic keeping the peace
with France, as President, in 1800, when every one was shouting for war;
and lastly, his struggle for religious liberty in Massachusetts in 1820, when
he was an old man of eighty-five.   Few men, boys and girls, can show
a better credit side on the ledger of fame than this honest, stanch, stout,
fussy, hot-tempered, but always fine old patriot, John Adams of Quincy,
second President of the United States."

"That is a pretty good record, I tell you," commented Bert, enthusiastically, while Jack doffed his hat, in sight of the gilded dome, and exclaimed, "Three cheers for the Father of the Fourth of July!"

That gilded dome, which had so frequently attracted their notice in Quincy town, topped the square, old-fashioned, and well-preserved "Stone Temple," otherwise the First Congregational (Unitarian) Church of Quincy, in which are the tombs of the two Presidents, father and son.

STATUARY HALL IN THE CAPITOL AT WASHINGTON.

The old House of Representatives, and the place where John Quincy Adams died.

The tourists looked at the space beneath the portico in which rest the remains of these two illustrious men ; they read the commemorative tablets set within the church to the right and left of the pulpit, one surmounted by a bust of John Adams, by Greenough, the other by a bust of John Quincy Adams, by Powers.

It was both interesting and impressive — "the Westminster Abbey of Quincy," Uncle Tom called it, and the young people left the quaint old church with renewed respect for the memories of the two famous Americans who lie buried there, within the church in which they worshiped, midway between the homes of their infancy and their old age. Somehow, even though the Adamses of Quincy were not soldiers, Christine said that she could not help repeating the lines :

> "How sleep the brave who sink to rest,
> By all their country's wishes blessed!"

Leaving the "temple," they walked up Hancock street, and just at the turn of Adams street looked at the neat stone building surmounted by an obelisk-like tower. This, Uncle Tom told them, was Adams Academy, founded by President John Adams, built on the site of John Hancock's birthplace, and presided over for many years by the son of Edward Everett.

"How's that for a combination?" asked Roger.

"I don't believe it makes lessons go any easier," declared Jack.

" As for John Quincy Adams," said Uncle Tom, continuing the "setting right" process, which Marian had requested, "we can say quite as much as for his father, although his career had not so historic a background. As a boy he went to school in France and Holland, while his father was abroad on foreign service for the new republic.   But he came back

THE HOUSE IN WHICH JOHN ADAMS DIED.
The "Old Charles Francis Adams" house, Quincy.

here of his own accord to enter Harvard because he thought that, for an American career, an American education was best."

" Good for him! " exclaimed the boys.

" Oh, he was quite a remarkable boy, was John Quincy Adams," Uncle Tom assured them.   " When only seven years old he drilled with a musket among the Continental soldiers, and I have told you how, from the top of Penn's Hill yonder, he stood beside his mother and watched the battle-smoke of Bunker Hill, the storming of Dorchester Heights, and the evacuation of Boston.   The good people of Quincy have just erected a cairn to mark the spot—that memorial pile of stones which I showed you on top of the hill, you know.   At ten he sailed with his father, the American 'commissioner,' to France, and all through his boyhood John Quincy Adams kept a diary that would be a surprise to some girls and boys I know."

CHARLES FRANCIS ADAMS.
United States Minister to England during the Civil War.

"He was private secretary to the American minister to Russia at four-teen," continued Uncle Tom. "He was minister to Holland at twenty-seven; minister to Prussia at thirty; United States senator at thirty-five; professor in Harvard at thirty-nine; minister to Russia at forty-two; minister to England at forty-eight; Secretary of State at fifty, and again at fifty-four; President of the United States at fifty-seven; member of Congress at sixty-four, continuing as such until his death at eighty — the champion of liberty, and a valiant fighter for the rights of free speech, whom no antagonist could daunt and no threats could down. A remarkable man, as

well as a remarkable boy, was John Quincy Adams — and that 's where he
lived, in that long brown mansion across the bridge, where lived also his
famous old father and his illustrious son."

"Oh, what a lovely old place!" exclaimed Marian. "Is n't it quaint
and old-fashioned. Who lives there now?"

"No one, I believe," replied Uncle Tom. "The place seems to be
closed. But it has been the scene of many interesting happenings. Here
old 'Grandsire John,' the 'first Adams,' lived and died; here John Quincy
Adams made his home, and delighted to work on his farm in 'overalls' and
a straw hat, like any other farmer, just as ready to receive a distinguished
visitor in his working clothes as if he were in the White House itself."

They crossed "the President's Bridge," which spans the railroad, and
entered the grounds now known as "the old Charles Francis Adams place";
they stood beneath the great trees, rested on the narrow piazza, visited the
modern stables and the long greenhouses, and walked about the wide fields
that stretched in the rear of the quaint gambrel-roofed house.

Then they slowly sauntered back to the center of the town, and as they
took the train for Boston, tired, but full of a new regard for these old
"fathers of the republic," Bert echoed Uncle Tom's sentiment and said:

"I guess you were right, Uncle Tom. Quincy granite may be enduring, but these Quincy men will outlast it — both in name and fame."

ADAMS ACADEMY, QUINCY.
Founded by John Adams, and built on the site of John Hancock's birthplace.

CHAPTER III

IN THE OLD COLONY

From Plymouth to Duxbury — The Puritan Captain — The Webster Farm — Marshfield By the Sea — Daniel Webster's Story — The Home of a Great American.

T HEY had spent two delightful days in historic Plymouth, and Uncle Tom declared himself to be fairly "pumped dry" on Colonial history.

"Dry!" exclaimed Jack, in his enthusiastic way. "That's not possible, Uncle Tom. You're like the fellow Mark Twain tells about: you just 'leak facts.' Only think of all we've seen and heard about during these last two days!"

"I should say so," said Bert. "We've done Plymouth from Leyden street to Billington Sea, and from the Rock and the Faith Monument to Lora Stan-

dish's sampler in Pilgrim Hall. And for everything we've seen, Uncle Tom, you had a story."

"Yes; only I told the story about Lora Standish's sampler, did n't I, Uncle Tom?" said Marian.

"You did, indeed, my dear," replied Uncle Tom. "Credit to whom credit is due, Master Bert. I see that you've read your Mrs.

PLYMOUTH ROCK AS IT LOOKS TO-DAY.

Austin to good effect, girls. Now, I suppose, you will go home and read 'Standish of Standish' with a new interest."

"That's more than I can do for Mrs. Hemans," declared Jack. "'Stern and rock-bound coast, 'eh? Why, the only rock they can show here is *the*, Rock — and that you say was a pilgrim from Labrador, Uncle Tom.   People ought to know what they write about."

"Well, Mrs. Hemans's intention was excellent, even if her facts were at fault," said Uncle Tom; "and 'the breaking waves' will continue to 'dash high' so long as spirited and noble verse strikes deep into the hearts of men.   We 've about finished Plymouth.   Now, I 'm going to take you back to Boston by a new way."

PLYMOUTH AND PLYMOUTH HARBOR FROM BURIAL HILL.

Uncle Tom always had a new way.

"He 's better than Columbus for discovering things," the boys and girls declared, and they were not surprised, therefore when, leaving famous old Plymouth behind, he said, "all out for Duxbury!" as the train slowed up at a neat little station ten miles nearer Boston.

They found a barge awaiting them — not a boat, you understand, like Cleopatra's famous float, but a long and roomy two-horse wagon, open at the sides — just the thing for a jolly party of sight-seers.

They drove in sight of the sea, with the Gurnet light gleaming white in the foreground, and the storied course of the *Mayflower* lying before them, sparkling in the sun.   They looked with proper pride upon the old Standish house, on the site of the one in which the valiant captain of Plymouth made his home; then they panted their way up the steep slope to the crest of

Captain's Hill, where rises the tall, gray column topped by a statue of the doughty leader of the Pilgrims' little army.

They drank in that splendid view of sea and shore; then, descending, they boarded their barge again, and rode through Duxbury town, past the home of John Alden and Priscilla — dear to all the boys and girls of America who delight in a charming love-story, and at last came to Marshfield and modern history. For Marshfield, so Uncle Tom told them, was the dearly loved home of Daniel Webster, foremost of American statesmen.

STANDISH HOUSE, DUXBURY, MASS.
Built by the son of Miles Standish, 1666.

The places they had visited, and the scenes amid which they had spent two memorable days in that famous "Old Colony" region, had made a lasting impression on their young and receptive minds. So, as their barge rolled along the new State Highway that, in time, will stretch all the way from Boston to Plymouth, the young people were still talking of the historic scenes they had left behind.

Jack and the girls, indeed, were holding an animated discussion as to the place of the Pilgrim Fathers in American history, to which Uncle Tom listened in amused silence. But when Jack, in his enthusiasm, placed gallant Miles Standish, "the Puritan captain," alongside Grant and Sherman in military supremacy, Uncle Tom felt it time to put in a word.

"Easy, easy, old fellow," he said, with a pat of caution on the boy's shoulder; "I 'm afraid your hero-worship of the moment is leading you into a bit of exaggeration. Miles Standish was a picturesque figure in

SWORD OF MILES STANDISH.
Of ancient Persian manufacture. In Pilgrim Hall.

early American history; but even he, I think, would smile in his quiet fashion if he could hear your estimate of his military ability."

"I don't see why, Uncle Tom," persisted Jack. "You said yourself that it was fortunate for America that one trained soldier came over in the *Mayflower;* and from what you told me of his story — "

"And what Longfellow says about him in the 'Courtship of Miles Standish,'" put in Marian.

"But Uncle Tom says that is more poetry than fact, you know," remarked Bert.

"I thought we had left the Pilgrim days and folks behind us, and had done with them for a while," said Uncle Tom, laughing. "The truth of the matter is here: Miles Standish was a notable figure in what the world now regards as a notable time. Hasty in temper, but never a coward — "

"Oh, I don't know about that, Uncle Tom," broke in Marian. "He was afraid of Priscilla."

"Afraid!" cried Jack, disdainfully.

"But Priscilla was n't afraid of him," Marian declared. "Don't you remember what she said about him?

"He is a little chimney and heated hot in a moment."

"I call that mighty mean of Priscilla, too," Jack spluttered. "Just like a girl! Lot she knew about a soldier!"

NO PLACE FOR A COWARD.

"No; she was right, was n't she, Uncle Tom?" returned Marian. "No girl likes to be treated as Miles Standish treated her. Lot he knew about a woman, I say!"

"See here, see here," protested Uncle Tom, laughing; "are we settling the facts of American history, or reopening the old Standish-Alden case?

Kindly restrain your impetuous partizanship, and let me finish summing up Miles Standish's character. Where was I?"

"You said he was never a coward, you know," prompted Bert.

"Oh, yes. Hasty in temper, but never a coward," again began Uncle Tom; "wise in counsel, but never foolhardy; trained to war, but never seeking a quarrel, he was especially fitted to teach the struggling and dis-pirited colonists of Plymouth the prudence of courage, the wisdom of discipline, and the excellence of vigilance. These, you see, are all qualities neces-sary in a military leader. They are what made Grant and Sherman successful generals. In fact, it may be said that in the single heroic person of Miles Standish was to be found the true soldierly idea — skilled military force in loyal subordi-nation to the civil authority. Miles Standish never sought to thrust himself forward; but when put in command by those in control, he did his duty faith-fully and well. He is indeed a typical Colonial soldier. As such, America should remem-

EDWARD WINSLOW.
By permission of the Massachusetts Historical Society.

ber and honor him; and it has been well for us to recall him, here, in the neighborhood where he grew into history."

They turned from the macadamized highway and into a sandy road, the note of the sea falling upon their ears in an unbroken monotone. They rode past the old house in which once had lived two famous governors of the Plymouth colony — Edward Winslow ("a greater than Standish," Uncle Tom declared) and Josiah, his son; past the home of a once famous Ameri-can songstress, rebuilt from the humble cottage of her poor farmer father, and then entered the grounds known to all the world as Marshfield — the two-thousand acre farm of America's statesman and orator, Daniel Webster.

There was not very much to see that could recall that remarkable man. The long avenue of trees that skirted the drive were of Webster's planting; the great apple orchard was of his devising; the trout-pond was of his plan-

DANIEL WEBSTER.

From a daguerreotype made in Philadelphia about 1849

ning; and here and there on the grounds — the farm, rather, for Webster
never called his place anything but a "farm" — were numerous localities
that were associated with the mighty man who delighted to be known as
"the farmer of Marshfield," and whose heart, even in the most engrossing
political moves and successes, ever turned toward his dearly loved seaside
farm, with its broad fields and sturdy trees, and the flocks and live stock in
which he specially delighted.

But the house which had been his home was not there.

The children were greatly disappointed when they learned this fact.

"Burned down, did you say, Uncle Tom?" inquired Roger.

"Yes; burned utterly and swiftly on a February night in 1878," Uncle
Tom replied. "This building is a modern villa, built by the new owners
of Marshfield to replace the old mansion. And with the old house went
many memories that would be of interest and value to-day. That little
yellow building, just across the drive to the left, is the sole survivor of the
old 'Webster place,' as they call it about here. In it Webster kept his
fishing and hunting traps, and called it his 'office.' That little 'office' and
the old carriage you can see in the barn yonder are about the only memorials
of Daniel Webster now to be seen at Marshfield. But the place — the setting
that framed his chosen home — still remains untouched by time — here are
the same blue sky, the same strong, health-giving air, the same landscape of
field and forest, the same ceaseless note of the sea across the marshes. All
these Webster loved; from these he drew vigor and inspiration, and toward
them he turned with an intense longing from crowded court-room and
senate chamber in which his fame was made."

Although scarcely the Marshfield of Webster's day, the children found
themselves impressed by the presence that once had filled this breezy
seaside farm. Seated upon the steps which, in the modern mansion, have
replaced the long, low vine-covered piazza of the rambling old homestead
destroyed by fire, the tourists fell to talking of the great man to whom
these broad acres had once belonged. In response to their inquiries Uncle
Tom briefly told his boys and girls the story of Daniel Webster's useful and
busy life.

He told them of the pale and puny baby born, on a January day in 1782,
into the home of a hard-working New Hampshire farmer; of the father,
Washington's trusted sentry at West Point in the dark days of Arnold's treason; of the boy's early struggles for an education, tempered by his resistless
love of fun; of his insatiable thirst for knowledge; of his school life at Exe-
ter Academy, where he was so shy that he found it impossible to speak "pieces"
before his schoolmates; of his wonderful eyes and yet more wonderful memory;

THE WEBSTER HOUSE AT MARSHFIELD.
Burned in February, 1878, and now replaced by a modern villa.

of his voice, so rich and full that the teamsters and farmers would stop the boy in the road to hear him recite poetry or verses from the Bible. He told them how Webster's father sacrificed everything to send his boy to Dartmouth College, and was rewarded by seeing his son the "prize student"; how his marvelous intellectual and oratorical powers gradually developed, until the boy orator of sixteen grew into the man whose matchless reply to Hayne has been called "the greatest speech since Demosthenes." He told them of Webster's election to Congress in 1822, and how, for twenty-eight years, he was Massachusetts's foremost representative in the councils of the nation, broken only by two seasons of service as Secretary of State, under Harrison, the fourteenth President, and Fillmore, the sixteenth. He told them of the great statesman's services to the nation, of his unfaltering love of country, of his absorbing belief in the greatness of the republic and its magnificent possibilities, and how valiantly he fought in argument and State paper and oration for the Union above everything else—for the integrity of the republic and the permanence of American nationality. It was this, even more than personal ambition, that worked Webster's downfall, so Uncle Tom declared, as he told his young auditors of the terrible shock with which Webster's famous speech of the 7th of March, 1850, supporting the wicked Fugitive Slave Law, fell upon his steadfast supporters. It was "the Union, now and forever, one and inseparable," so Uncle Tom assured them, that lay beneath even this unfortunate speech. But the statesman was misunderstood. That speech lost Webster the Presidency, which he so dearly desired; it turned

against him the men of the North, to whom he looked for approval and support; it so affected him, because of the results, that, two years later, on
the 24th of October, 1852, the great statesman died here, in quiet Marshfield, the victim of his own mistaken judgment and the equally mistaken
judgment of his fellow-citizens.

JOHN GREENLEAF WHITTIER.
The Poet of Freedom.

"But why do you call it mistaken, Uncle Tom?" asked Bert, who had
followed the narrative with close attention. "Do you call Whittier's 'Ichabod' poem mistaken — the one you told us about in Boston, you know?"

"Let Whittier answer himself, Bert," replied Uncle Tom. "He wrote the
'Ichabod' poem in 1850, when the antislavery indignation at Webster's sup-

posed backsliding was at white heat. Beneath the regret and grief you can read his fiery denunciation. But, after twenty-five years had passed, with

EVENING ON THE MARSHES.

all their marvelous changes, and yet more marvelous advancement, Whittier, looking back, could say that Webster had died too soon, and that, had he lived, he would have been the boldest defender of the liberty he had mistakenly imperiled. Let me see if I can remember Whittier's lines. They make a grand poem on Webster — 'The Lost Occasion' was what the poet called it"; and Uncle Tom, leaning his head against the piazza post, closed his eyes and recited the noble lines by Whittier to which he referred:

"Thou, foiled in aim and hope, bereaved
Of old friends, by the new deceived,
Too soon for us, too soon for thee,
Beside thy lonely Northern sea,
Where long and low the marsh-lands spread,
Laid wearily down thy august head.

Thou shouldst have lived to feel below
Thy feet Disunion's fierce upthrow,—
The late-sprung mine that underlaid
Thy sad concessions, vainly made.
Thou shouldst have seen from Sumter's wall
The star-flag of the Union fall,
And armed rebellion pressing on
The broken lines of Washington!
No stronger voice than thine had then
Called out the utmost might of men,
To make the Union's charter free
And strengthen law by liberty.

How had that stern arbitrament
To thy gray age youth's vigor lent,
Shaming ambition's paltry prize
Before thy disillusioned eyes;

Breaking the spell about thee wound
Like the green withes that Samson bound;
Redeeming in one effort grand,
Thyself and thy imperiled land.

Ah, cruel fate, that closed to thee,
O sleeper by the Northern sea,
The gates of opportunity!
God fills the gaps of human need,
Each crisis brings its word and deed.
Wise men and strong we did not lack,
But still, with memory turning back,
In the dark hours we thought of thee,
And thy lone grave beside the sea."

Uncle Tom rose to his feet.

"Come, let us go and see that 'lone grave'," he said.

He led the way past the great barn, with its double line of just such noble stock as Webster loved, and on, across the farm, to where, half a mile away, upon the crest of Burial Hill, stood the old Colonial burying-ground. There were buried the Winslows of Colonial days; there was the grave of Peregrine White, first child of the *Mayflower* pilgrims; and there, within

THE GRAVE OF WEBSTER.
" Just *'Daniel Webster'*—that 's all."

the Webster plot, the children looked upon the modest marble slab which marks the statesman's grave.

"Simple enough, is n't it?" said Roger. "Just *Daniel Webster*—that 's all."

ON THE ROAD TO MARSHFIELD.

The oldest meeting-house in New England (Hingham, Mass.).

"Seems to me so great a man as Webster ought to have more of a monument," was Jack's critical comment.

"I don't know," mused Bert. "Somehow you get nearer to a man just as he was by such a simple thing as that; don't you think so, Uncle Tom? That name tells it all. You know who Daniel Webster was. What more do you need? Really, don't you know, to me it seems grander than all those long-winded inscriptions on the Adams tablets at Quincy."

Jack was still unconvinced.

"If you 're big enough to be remembered, you 're worth saying something about," he insisted.

And Uncle Tom said: "I like to have you see and study these memorials of departed greatness, boys and girls. I think I 'm on Bert's side of the argument, however. For, after all, a man's life-work is his best monument. What he does for the world and his fellow-men will last longer than granite or bronze. Some of the biggest monuments have been built above the smallest memories. To my thinking, Daniel Webster, as Bert says, needs no other memorial than this modest stone. He has built himself into the hearts and life of the people. How many of you know his famous reply to Hayne?"

At once every boy and girl of the five began that famous peroration: "When my eyes shall be turned to behold for the last time the sun in heaven — '"

"That's it," said Uncle Tom, cutting them short. "Do you suppose you can ever forget who spoke those electric words? As Bert says, we all know who Daniel Webster was. His country has honored him. His statue, in marble or in bronze, stands in our greatest cities; his name is inwrought with the daily life of our land — counties, townships, institutions, parks, streets, lakes, mountains, and men alike bear his honored name; but more than this, the eloquent words he spoke for liberty and union, for American nationality and American supremacy, will live ás long as the English language exists and school-boys live to speak it. There was nothing sectional, nothing small in his patriotism; above all else, Daniel Webster was an American."

"Did n't he say so in one of his speeches?" asked Christine.

"' I was born an American; I live an American; I shall die an American,'" quoted Roger.

"That was in a speech soon after the famous 7th of March oration that so clouded his fame," explained Uncle Tom, "and it explains much in his career. For that was his creed, and to advance the interests of America was his chief desire. Indeed, he was in his way a type of American greatness. He was great himself, physically and intellectually. He loved great things: this view, over marsh and sea, and farm and forest, especially appealed to him — "

"It is great," exclaimed Jack, appreciatively.

"He loved bigness in everything — big farms, big trees, big cattle, mountains, Niagara, the ocean; and for that reason, as I have said, he could stand nothing small or sectional or local in American life. He loved the Union as a whole; he be-

WEBSTER'S CHAIR AND WALKING-STICK.
Now at Marshfield.

lieved in and labored for its immense possibility; and in trying to preserve it unbroken, he made what at the time appeared to be the great mistake of his life. But the lapse of years creates a new standpoint, you know, and as we look back on Webster's life and Webster's work, we can see that all, even what men counted as his error, worked to a good end."

DANIEL WEBSTER'S BIRTHPLACE IN SALISBURY (NOW FRANKLIN), N. H.
He was born in the extension, or ell, on the eighteenth of January, 1782.

"There 's your Pope again, Uncle Tom," said Bert —

"From seeming evil still educing good."

"Right you are, Bert," returned Uncle Tom; "only, as I told you once before, my Pope was Thomson."

"That 's what you call a word in season, eh, Uncle Tom?" said Jack, slyly.

But Uncle Tom caught him by the arm. "If you will make puns, old fellow, make correct ones," he replied. "I should call it a word out of season —for it happens to be not from Thomson's 'Seasons,' but from one of his hymns." Whereat the others, who were a bit puzzled by this literary sparring, saw the fun at last, and declared that the joke was on Master Jack.

As they walked back to the house and to their waiting barge, Bert, always alert for estimates and judgments, asked Uncle Tom what he considered Webster's greatest triumphs. To which Uncle Tom replied that, in the estimation of historians, the treaty with England in 1842, when Webster was Secretary of State, and the reply to Hayne, in 1830, were Webster's strongest claims to remembrance and immortality. The first was a triumph of diplomacy, the second a triumph of oratory.

" Because of the treaty," declared Uncle Tom, " England never again attempted the right of search, which had twice imperiled the republic ; because of the speech, came the new United States—the real Union of to-day. I do not think it too much to say," he added, " that because Webster's ' Liberty and Union' oration became the favorite declamation of American school-boys in the fifties, it inspired a devoted and passionate love for the Union, which, when the hour of danger came to the republic, emphasized the sentiment of nationality, and nerved the arm, as it sustained the courage, of the united North. In that, as Senator Lodge says, lies the debt which the American people owe to Daniel Webster, and in that is Webster's meaning and importance to us of to-day.

" And it may interest and please you to know, boys and girls," he continued, as once again they stood near the site of Webster's Marshfield home, " that from the window of the house which formerly stood upon this spot, Webster, when he lay a-dying, looked out each morning to catch the flutter of the stars and stripes which he so dearly loved, and which, according to his orders, were kept floating from the flagstaff until his last breath passed. Does that recall anything to you in the way of a coincidence?"

JOHN HOWARD PAYNE.
One of Webster's foreign appointments when he was Secretary of State.
Consul at Tunis in 1841. Author of " Home, Sweet Home."

They hesitated a moment; then Jack, quick to see and appreciate such dramatic things, cried :

"Oh, yes, Uncle Tom ; don't you know—" and then, before Webster's home, on the very spot where so many of the happy moments of his life were passed, close beside the place where, with eyes wet with tears, the great orator penned his splendid eulogy on Adams and Jefferson in the still hours of a summer morning, Jack recited, as Jack knew so well how to recite, the words that will live as long as the name and fame of their author shall survive :

" When my eyes shall be turned to behold for the last time the sun in heaven, may I not see him shining on the broken and dishonored fragments of a once glorious Union; on States dissevered, discordant, belligerent; on a land rent with civil feuds, or drenched, it may be, in fraternal blood. Let their last feeble and lingering glance rather behold the gorgeous ensign of the republic, now known and honored throughout the earth, still full high advanced, its arms and trophies streaming in their original lustre, not a stripe erased nor polluted, not a single star obscured, bearing for its motto no such miserable interrogatory as ' What is all this worth ? ' — nor those other words of delusion and folly, ' Liberty first and Union afterwards ! '; but everywhere, spread all over in characters of living light, blazing on all its ample folds as they float over the sea and over the land, and in every wind under the whole heavens, that other sentiment dear to every American heart : ' Liberty and Union, now and forever, one and inseparable ! ' "

"And it happened just as he wished, did n't it?" said Christine, stirred by the magnificent words and the associations of the place where she stood.

"It happened just as he wished," replied Uncle Tom. " He saw the flag floating undimmed to the last. And on yonder lawn, before his house, beneath the great silver poplar which he loved, now standing no longer, thousands came on a beautiful October day in 1852, to look their last upon the face of the great statesman whom Theodore Parker described as the grandest figure in Christendom since Charlemagne. He lay there, banked in flowers, dead, beneath the autumn sky. But, from that sad hour to these happier days of the republic's real liberty and real union, the fame of Daniel Webster has steadily increased until the world looks upon him not only as a great man, but as in the best sense an American, a real son of the republic, a citizen of the United States, in the most complete and most enduring meaning of that noble word. Forget his faults, remember his virtues, boys and girls, and be, as long as life shall last, as true an American and as loyal a child of the republic as was Daniel Webster, to whose great heart, mighty brain, and magnetic voice you young Americans of this day owe so much."

CHAPTER IV

New York's Greatest Man — A Tour of the Old Town — Famous Men and Historic Points — The Story of Alexander Hamilton — A Remarkable Character.

EW YORK'S greatest man?" said Uncle Tom, reflectively, in answer to a question from Roger. "Why, I should say, without hesitation, Alexander Hamilton — even if we count General Grant."

"General Grant!" cried the Boston boy. "Why, how do you make that out, Uncle Tom? Grant was an Illinois man, I thought."

"Primarily, yes," Uncle Tom replied; "though he was Ohio-born, you know. But we are regarding America's famous men after they had become, as we might say, the property of the nation. Grant was practically a cipher until developed into greatness by the inspiration of war. After the war and the Presidency, New York was his chosen home; so, for our purpose, we can, I think, claim him as a New York man. At any rate, I prefer so to consider him at this stage of the inquiry; for, except for Grant and Hamilton, another adopted citizen, New York can lay claim to few really historic characters, and to still less really great ones. Men drift here from one reason or another, and thus become identified with the metropolis; but the native has never been exceptional for greatness."

They were in New York. Roger had come on for a visit, and Uncle Tom, finding his tourists all together and eager for investigation, had proposed a continuation of their study of famous Americans, suggesting a trip to Philadelphia after they had paid their respects to New York.

From this had sprung Roger's query and Uncle Tom's reply. Jack, however, objected with true Knickerbocker loyalty.

"Oh, see here, Uncle Tom," he cried, "you must be wrong. I'll bet I can name a dozen great men who were New Yorkers."

JOHN JAY

"Name them, Jack, and I'll forgive the bet," returned Uncle Tom. "I'm listening with avidity."

Jack hesitated. "Well," he said slowly, "if I were as well posted as you are, I could do so. I know I could; but you know, Uncle Tom, I've got an awfully good forgettery."

The other boys were inclined to charge Jack with something technically known in boy language as a "crawl," and Uncle Tom laughed heartily.

"Well, let me help you, Jack," he said. "Recollect that our particular line of research is *great* Americans; and by greatness I mean popular adoption — the people's stamp of greatness. When you attempt that test you can count all the really great Americans on your ten fingers. There are others ——"

GOV. GEORGE CLINTON.

"Here, here, Uncle Tom," laughed Jack, "you are dropping into slang, too. We'll have to take you in hand, sir."

"Why, what did I say?" asked Uncle Tom. "It's all your fault, Jack. 'Evil communications corrupt good manners,' you know. Among historic Americans, New York city can claim many: John Jay, first Chief Justice of the United States, a patriot and a statesman; the two Clintons, George and DeWitt, kinsmen and governors; the two Livingstons, Robert and Edward, brothers, jurists and statesmen. These are names high on New York's roll of fame, but I fear they must all yield precedence in greatness to the two historic names I have given you as heading the list — Hamilton and Grant. Anyhow, we'll go out and investigate."

They did so, next day. Wise Uncle Tom selected a Sunday morning before church time, and after a particularly early breakfast, for his first walk. Then he knew lower Broadway would virtually be deserted, and they could wander through the old streets at their will without being pushed or jostled by the hurrying and unhistoric crowds of a busy week day.

ROBERT R. LIVINGSTON.

So, with Uncle Tom as guide, the five investigators walked the ancient section of the old town which Dutch traders had founded, and English

"HERE PETER STUYVESANT PLAYED THE DESPOT."

traders had developed, and American traders had made great. Up and down
those very streets, years and years before, men whose names are familiar, or
whose lives are notable, had walked and talked and labored. Here Wouter
Van Twiller had played the fool, and Peter Stuyvesant the despot; here
Kidd the pirate had lived like a gentleman, and Andros the dragoon had
ruled as governor; here Jacob Leisler, earliest of American patriots, had died
for popular liberty, and Zenger, New York's first "newspaper man," had
fought for the right of free speech, and obtained it.

They threaded the crooked streets of the old town, and tried to imagine
what it looked like in the days of beginnings when Wall street was really
"the street along the wall," and Pearl street was "the Strand," or river beach.
In fancy, they pulled down the towering modern building at 39 Broadway,
and put in its place the two little huts built by Block's shipwrecked sailors
—first homes of the white man in New York. They stood on the breezy
Battery, reminder of the vigorous Leisler, who gave it its name; they located
the circle of the ancient fort which had witnessed so many momentous
scenes, but none more notable than the bold adoption of the colonists'
"charter of liberties" in 1683.

Here, at the corner of Pearl and Whitehall streets, they located the
house in which had lived Leisler, the people's governor, and recalled his

VIEW OF FEDERAL HALL, 1797.
Where Washington was inaugurated.

dramatic story; there, near at hand, had stood the queer old "Stadt Huys," or City Hall, where aristocracy and democracy had waged their earliest battles.

It was all very interesting, because, as Christine said, it was making over the past, and if you could only unthink, as she expressed it, all the real brick and granite and iron, you could imagine the quaint old houses and odd surroundings of the place as they looked in Washington's day.

Uncle Tom helped them to " unthink " the modern dress.

" Call it Washington's day," he said. " New York is the capital of the new republic, and many of the great ones of that storied time live hereabouts. Yonder, on Pearl street, near Wall, are the houses of Livingston and Clinton; not far away Chief-Justice Jay keeps open house; on Maiden Lane lives Jefferson, while Hamilton, his great rival, is on Wall street; and here, in front of No. 1 Broadway, which is President Washington's residence, you may perhaps catch a glimpse of these two great statesmen walking up and down for a full half hour, talking earnestly together as, between themselves, they arrange for the selection of the site of the new capital of the United States — the city of Washington that is to be."

" I declare, Uncle Tom, I can almost see them now," Marian announced.

Then, by a wide loop in their walk, Uncle Tom showed his young people the spot where, at the close of the Revolution, plucky Jack Van Arsdale, the sailor boy, climbed the greased pole on the battery and flung out the stars and stripes in the face of the departing British. He paused with them

before Ward's splendid statue of Washington on the sub-Treasury steps —
the very spot on which he took the oath of office as President; he showed
them the region of "Golden
Hill" on John street, near Cliff,
where the first blood of the
Revolution was spilled, while
not far away, in the sparkling
harbor, he pointed out the place
where New York's "tea party"
had been held; he took them to
City Hall Park, and pointed out
where Jacob Leisler had been
martyred for independence and
Nathan Hale for liberty; he
crossed the street and pointed

OLD CITY HALL, WALL STREET, 1776.

out the tomb of Montgomery, the hero of Quebec, set in the brown front
of St. Paul's, and let them stand for an instant within the old church,
in the very pew which had been Washington's. Then, passing down
the street, they came to Trinity churchyard. There, with minds now

"A PROSPECTIVE VIEW OF THE CITY HALL IN NEW YORK,
TAKEN FROM WALL STREET."
From a print in possession of the New York Historical Society.

thoroughly in what Uncle Tom called "an historic mood," they surveyed
the brown sarcophagus that shrines the remains of "Don't-give-up-the-
ship" Lawrence, as Jack designated him; they found the sunken slab

that covers the grave of poor Charlotte Temple; they stood before the towering obelisk that stands as a memorial "to those great and good men who died while imprisoned in this city for their devotion to the cause of American Independence"; and so came at last to the modest gray monu-

ment on the south side of Trinity churchyard beneath which rest the bones of one of the greatest of historic Americans and of famous men — Alexander Hamilton.

Bert read the inscription on the base: "'To the memory of Alexander Hamilton, the corporation of Trinity Church has erected this monument in testimony of their respect for the Patriot of incomparable integrity, the Soldier of approved valour, the Statesman of consummate wisdom, whose talents and virtues will be admitted by grateful posterity, long after this marble shall have mouldered into dust. He died July 12, 1804, aged 47.'"

The boys and girls regarded the inscription with interest. It seemed a fitting culmination to all they had seen that morning.

"Only forty-seven!" was Christine's comment. "He was n't so very old, was he? And he did so much."

"Somehow I always think of those Revolutionary fellows as old men," said Jack. "Don't you know how the song goes:

> "In their ragged regimentals
> Stood the old Continentals
> Yielding not.

But this does n't seem so, does it? Hamilton was an 'old Continental,' was n't he, Uncle Tom?"

"One of the earliest and youngest," replied Uncle Tom. "But then you must remember, Jack, that it is the young men who make history, and — govern yourself accordingly! Why, the average age of the fifty-six signers of the Declaration of Independence was only forty-four; twenty of them were under forty, and one was but twenty-four. Twenty of the signers of the Constitution were under forty — Madison and Hamilton, its authors and 'fathers,' were but thirty-six and thirty respectively. Age, you see, is not a requirement to statesmanship, and the remarkable story of Alexander Hamilton, before whose early grave we are standing, is proof of this."

"Did n't we hear something about him in Washington?" inquired Marian.

"To be sure we did — in the State Department, was n't it?" rejoined Christine.

"Why, yes," said Roger; "don't you remember when the custodian in the library showed us the real simon-pure original Constitution of the United States he told us about Hamilton and said that his story was one to make young men proud of their youth?"

"What do you recollect of his story, boys?" asked Uncle Tom.

"Let 's see," hesitated Bert, "the man in the State Department told us that Hamilton was an orator and patriot at seventeen, a hero at twenty, a statesman at twenty-three."

"Sort of 'historic boy,' eh, Uncle Tom?" suggested Jack.

"But was he all that so young?" Marian demanded.

"All that and more," Uncle Tom replied. "Alexander Hamilton was really, Jack, one of the world's his-

THE TOMB OF ALEXANDER HAMILTON.
In Trinity churchyard.

toric — one of its remarkable boys. Let me see if I can recall his record: At twelve, a confidential clerk in a mercantile house; at thirteen, man-

THE STATUE OF NATHAN HALE.
By Frederick McMonnies, recently erected in City Hall Park, New York.

ager; at fourteen, a descriptive writer; at sixteen, a regular student in college and at the same time taking a medical course; at seventeen, a popular orator; at nineteen, a captain of artillery in the Continental army; at twenty, a lieutenant-colonel and Washington's aide-de-camp; at twenty-three, a battalion commander; at twenty-four, a member of Congress; at thirty, framer and signer of the Constitution of the United States; at thirty-two, the first Secretary of the Treasury; at thirty-five, a great lawyer; at forty, a major-general; at forty-two, commander-in-chief of the armies of the United States; at forty-five, America's leading statesman; and at forty-seven — here, murdered by his relentless rival, Aaron Burr."

"Really murdered, Uncle Tom? How dreadful!" exclaimed Christine.

"I thought he was killed in a duel," said Jack. "Duelling was n't called murder then."

"He must have been murdered," said Roger, solemnly. "I know a verse my grandmother used to tell me. She got it from her father, she said. How did it go? — something like this:

> "O Aaron Burr, what have you done?
> You 've shot poor General Hamilton.
> You got behind a bunch of thistles
> And shot him dead with two horse-pistols."

"Oh, see here, that is n't history, is it?" exclaimed Bert.

Uncle Tom laughed.

"Current tradition done into doggerel," he said. "It was n't just like that, Roger, although, as I said, duelling is murder, and in this instance it was deliberate murder, even without the thistles and horse-pistols of your great-grandfather's rhyme. Burr was determined to kill Hamilton, while Hamilton fired his pistol in the air, simply wanting to follow out the form of a duel without its tragic ending. But if it killed Hamilton, physically, it killed Burr, morally and politically, for it proved to be the greatest mistake of his mistaken and wrongly balanced life. It rounded out Hamilton's fame, and drove Burr into treason and ignominy."

As they turned from the grave of one of America's most brilliant statesmen, and took the cable car up Broadway for home, Uncle Tom rehearsed briefly Hamilton's remarkable story:

"Hamilton was born in 1757 on the island of Nevis, one of—who knows where Nevis is?" he asked.

They were good geography scholars and not to be caught napping.

"One of the Leeward Islands, down Venezuela way," said Bert.

"Yes, and an English possession," added Uncle Tom. "Well, there

WASHINGTON'S PEW IN ST. PAUL'S CHURCH AS IT IS TO-DAY.

Alexander Hamilton was born in 1757, and before he was ten years old had to look out for himself. He was a remarkably bright boy even then; he had ambitions and aspirations, and told his boy friends he meant to be somebody in the world when he grew up. Before he was in his teens he became the confidential clerk of his employer, a merchant in the distant island of Santa Cruz; there, too, he wrote and read a great deal and showed so much talent that friends sent him to the northern colonies for an education. He went to school in New Jersey and then to King's College (now Columbia). In 1774 he made a visit to Boston, and heard so much talk about liberty that he came back to New York a full-fledged patriot —"

"Boston air," asserted Roger in an aside to Jack; "that's the effect it has on New Yorkers."

"Is that so?" drawled Jack. "Why, my son, Golden Hill came two months before the Boston massacre; Uncle Tom said so."

But Uncle Tom had not caught this side sparring and was going on with his story.

"Soon after his return, in an open-air mass meeting where he thought the speakers were not convincing enough, Hamilton, then a boy of seventeen, sprang to his feet and made a 'spur-of-the-moment' speech that set all his hearers on fire and brought him at once into favor as a popular orator.

ALEXANDER HAMILTON.
From the painting by Trumbull, 1792; now owned by the New York Chamber of Commerce.

When war really came, Hamilton enlisted at once. He led an artillery company at the battle of Long Island, and soon attracted the attention of Washington, who added him to his staff as an aide-de-camp. He fought through the Revolution, led the last charge at Yorktown, where Cornwallis surrendered, and came out of it all as Colonel Hamilton, aged twenty-five."

"My, though! he was a smart one, was n't he?" said Marian.

"Yes; he might have been a great soldier and a famous one," said Uncle

Tom, "if he had not made a still higher record as a statesman. He had a remarkable mind, you understand, and saw, even before older and more experienced men recognized it, the need of something reliable and binding if the Colonies were to be a real nation. When he was twenty-four, in a letter to a friend, he outlined many of the provisions that, seven years later, found place in the Constitution."

"I remember the man in the State Department told us that," said Bert. "Great, was n't it?"

"I tell you, Alexander was quite a boy," Jack declared impressively.

ONE RESULT OF HAMILTON'S IMPROMPTU SPEECH.
Tearing down the King's arms.

"After the Revolution," continued Uncle Tom, "Hamilton began business as a lawyer here in New York, but gave up his practice to go to Congress, and, later, to become a member of the convention that drafted and adopted the new Constitution of the United States, of which, as I have said, he was largely the father and framer. When the new nation was fairly on its feet, President Washington made Hamilton Secretary of the Treasury, and it was this wonderful financier of thirty-two who saved the young republic from bankruptcy and failure. Did any of you ever hear what Daniel Webster said of Hamilton and his services to the republic as Secretary of the Treasury?"

No one seemed to remember, and Uncle Tom quoted Webster's famous words, from his eulogy on Hamilton in 1831:

"He smote the rock of the national resources, and abundant streams of revenue gushed forth. He touched the dead corpse of Public Credit, and it sprung upon its feet."

"That's fine, is n't it!" exclaimed Jack. "Say, boys, D. W. knew how to put things, did n't he?"

"A great man always makes strong enemies, just as he creates faithful followers," continued Uncle Tom. "Hamilton was the object alike of the deepest admiration and the most bitter hatred. Chief among his enemies was Aaron Burr, a bold, shrewd, vindictive, and unscrupulous political 'boss' of that time. He knew that Hamilton saw through his schemes, fathomed his ambitions, and intended to thwart his designs. He set deliberately to work to fasten a quarrel upon Hamilton and kill him. He succeeded, and the famous and tragic duel across the river yonder, on the Weehawken shore, ended the earthly career of Hamilton, but raised him, as I have told you, to a pinnacle of fame which stands out all the bolder and more gloriously as the years go by. The man who thought out the Constitution of the United States, and the way in which the new nation should be firmly established and successfully 'run,' is not likely to fade from the grateful memories of the citizens of the great republic he prophesied and prepared for. That ends my lecture, boys and girls. Here's our corner. Now for home and morning church."

A day or two after this journey in patriotic paths, Uncle Tom took his young people far up-town on the west side of Manhattan Island. He pointed out to them the crest of the hill where was fought the battle of Harlem Heights, in which the young artillery captain Hamilton first attracted the attention of Washington, and where now rise the walls of the magnificent successor to that young patriot's modest college — then King's, now the new Columbia.

Soon they crested another hill, and stood at last amid the continually rising city mansions of this sightly part of upper New York — Convent Avenue between 142d and 143d streets.

Midway in this block, on the western side of Convent Avenue, Uncle Tom came to a standstill, and pointing to a clump of rather scraggy and slanting trees closely bunched together, said:

"Count them!"

"Thirteen," announced Roger. "What are they?"

"These thirteen trees," said Uncle Tom, impressively, "were planted by Alexander Hamilton to commemorate the union of the thirteen American colonies into a nation, after the adoption of the Constitution, in which he had so important a share. They have lasted thus long. They are now the property of the city. Let us hope the advance of population will not smother or overthrow these last memorials of the home of Alexander Hamilton."

TREES PLANTED BY HAMILTON.
Convent Avenue, New York.

"Why, was this his home?" inquired Marian.

"The Grange, Hamilton's country house, stood just to the left of that clump of trees," said Uncle Tom. "Now it has been removed. There it stands across the way, next to that Episcopal church."

With much interest the boys and girls looked across the avenue where, on the eastern side, stood the removed and renovated homestead of Hamilton, which he so dearly loved, and from which he had gone direct to his death that fatal 11th of July, 1804.

Jack shook his head meditatively, as if he too were recalling Hamilton's tragic story.

"It was a great shame," he said emphatically. "What a pity! I suppose there always are two sides to a story, and there may have been lots of outs about Hamilton — but I don't care; he was a great man, and I say three cheers for him."

"We are none of us perfect, Jack," said Uncle Tom; "but I am trying to show you young folks, in our great Americans, the things to remember,

not the things to forget. Alexander Hamilton was born to be great.
Marshall, our foremost Chief Justice, ranked him next to Washington. No
man has made a deeper mark on American history, or is entitled to a more
exalted station in the remembrance of the republic. He was a great orator,

THE HAMILTON GRANGE.
On Convent Avenue, New York; now a school.

a great lawyer, the ablest politician and statesman of his day, a fine soldier,
an organizer without a rival. Whatever he touched he mastered, and if
ever he made a mistake he was not afraid to say so. But though sometimes mistaken, he never failed. Hamilton's name stands for success, and
his story should be an inspiration to the boys and girls of America, for it
shows them that worthy ambition rightly pursued brings to men merited
success and enduring fame."

"Albert, my son," said Jack, patting his cousin on the head, "be a
Hamilton."

THE DUEL.

JOHN NIXON READING THE DECLARATION OF INDEPENDENCE IN
THE STATE HOUSE YARD, PHILADELPHIA, JULY 8, 1776.

CHAPTER V

THE HOME OF THE LIBERTY BELL

Where Franklin lived — An Extraordinary Man — The Story of a Helpful Life — Landmarks and Relics — Independence Hall and the Liberty Bell.

NCLE Tom stopped short and glanced about him.

"It must have been somewhere near this very spot," he said, "that a certain runaway Boston boy once did that difficult act, referred to in Boston by my friend Jack, of walking along with a roll under each arm, eating a third, and at the same time 'casting sheep's eyes' at a girl on the front stoop."

At once Jack thrust, first, a guide-book, and then a newspaper under Roger's arms, and forced a banana into his hand.

"Try it on, Roger," he said. "You 'll answer for the runaway Boston boy. Christine, you go stand in that doorway. We 'll make the whole Franklin story realistic."

But neither Roger nor Christine appeared to enter heartily into the spirit of what Jack styled his "realistic reproduction of an historic event," and Uncle Tom hurried the laughing group up Market street; for they were abroad, investigating old-time Philadelphia.

Suddenly he stopped again. Midway in the block between Third and Fourth streets, on the southern side of Market, he spied a queer, arched passage, and at once dived into it, followed by his wondering companions.

The alleyway widened as they advanced. Half way toward Chestnut street Uncle Tom stopped a third time.

"Here, boys and girls," he said, "once stood the house of the most extraordinary of Americans — Benjamin Franklin."

"Most extraordinary place to have a house," declared Bert.

"Here, in the middle of this block of the back doors of buildings, Uncle Tom?" cried Marian. "How funny!"

"THE GIRL AT WHOM HE 'CAST SHEEP'S EYES.'"

" As if they were here then, goosey !" exclaimed Jack.

Warehouses and blank walls hedged in the narrow court. It was neither attractive nor suggestive; but in Uncle Tom's eyes it was a shrine before which all patriotic Americans could stand with feelings of reverence.

The queer, narrow cut ran through the block from Market to Chestnut streets, and midway, so Uncle Tom assured them, had stood the house where Franklin lived with his dearly loved wife Deborah.

" The girl at whom he cast sheep's eyes while doing the three-loaves act, was n't she ?" inquired Jack.

" The same," said Uncle Tom —" Miss Deborah Read. Nothing remains of that house now. But from here went out truths that instructed the world; from here went the philosopher with his kite and his son into the fields beyond the town to experiment with the lightning — the pioneer of electrical science."

" That makes me think of that statue of him in front of the Electricity Building at the World's Fair," said Marian, " with his kite and all, you know."

STATUE OF BENJAMIN FRANKLIN.
Made for the Electricity Building, World's Fair Grounds, Chicago, 1893, and
now on the grounds of the University of Pennsylvania.

"He was a pioneer in many other things too, was he not?" inquired Bert.

"Indeed he was," Uncle Tom replied. "I know of no case in history of a man with equal genius for 'starting things.' Let me see if I can give you a list of the things which Benjamin Franklin set afloat."

Uncle Tom stood in the shade of a warehouse doorway, and ran over the list:

"He improved the printing-press, and introduced stereotyping and manifold letter-writers; he cured chimneys of smoking; bettered the shape and rig of ships; showed sailors the practical use of the Gulf Stream, and told them how to keep provisions fresh at sea. He improved soup-plates for men and water-troughs for beasts; he drained swamp-lands, and made them fertile and fruitful; he improved fireplaces, and invented stoves; he showed how to heat public buildings, and invented automatic fans to cool hot rooms and to keep off flies; he made double spectacles for far- and near-sighted folks; he invented a musical instrument, and improved an electrical machine; he taught men that lightning was electricity, relieved it of its terrors, and harnessed it to do the will of man; he invented lightning-rods, and was the first advocate of electrocution for killing animals instantly and without pain; he thought out phonography and shorthand; improved carriage wheels, wind-mills, and water-wheels; he revolutionized the covering of roofs; he invented sidewalks and crossing-stones,— at least for Philadelphia,— and showed that streets could be swept and kept clean. He founded the first philosophical society in America, the first improvement club, the first free schools outside of New England, the first public library, the first fire company, and the first periodical magazine. He started the Philadelphia police force and the first volunteer militia. He introduced the idea of humanity in war; protected the Indians; founded the first

FROM A FRENCH MEMORIAL TO FRANKLIN.
"He snatched the thunderbolt from heaven and the scepter from tyrants."

anti-slavery society; and introduced into America, from Europe, seeds, vines, and vegetables new to the Western world. That's a pretty good record of first things, is n't it? I don't believe you can match it in the history of the world."

"Whew! what a head he must have had!" said Jack. "Did he ever eat and sleep?"

"Well, I guess!" exclaimed Bert. "He's the fellow you've had to go to bed by, many a time. Don't you know that Franklin was the man who said:

"Early to bed and early to rise
Makes a man healthy, wealthy, and wise.

Is n't that so, Uncle Tom?"

"Certainly it is," his uncle replied. "Benjamin Franklin was the author and maker of 'Poor Richard's Almanack,' from which that rhyme comes, and which did more to influence public opinion in America than all the speeches of all the orators. It was full of just such thrifty maxims and wise counsels as Bert has just quoted — simple verses telling a great truth that parents would repeat and children would always remember. Franklin published his almanac annually for twenty-five years, and one student of history has declared that the battles of the American Revolution could not have been fought between 1775 and 1783 if 'Poor Richard's Almanack' had not been published from 1732 to 1758. There were hundreds and hundreds of homes in the American colonies in which the families knew and possessed only two books — the Bible for Sunday reading, and 'Poor Richard's Almanack' for the other six days of the week. As you can see from Master Bert here, people are quoting from it yet, though it stopped publication almost a hundred and fifty years ago."

"POOR RICHARD'S ALMANACK"

Title-page of the only existing copy of the first number, now in the possession of the Pennsylvania Historical Society, Philadelphia.

B. Franklin

, Interested, thus, in the remarkable man who for many years was so closely identified with American history and the progress of the world, the man who, as his French admirers affirmed, "snatched the thunderbolt from heaven and the scepter from tyrants," the young people followed Uncle Tom from the narrow confines of Franklin alley along what Jack afterward referred to as "the trail of B. Franklin."

They found signs of it in many quarters. They saw the great and beneficent Pennsylvania Hospital founded by him. Tucked away behind modern and obtrusive buildings they found, on Fourth street, between Market and Arch, the first school building of the University of Pennsylvania, started by Franklin in 1751. They visited the Philadelphia Library, organized by him in 1731; they saw the place where he helped Jefferson draft the Declaration of Independence, the place where he argued for it, the table on which he signed it, and the room in which he advocated and signed the Constitution of the United States. In the rooms of the American Philosophical Association, a scientific society founded by him, they were privileged to see certain cherished memorials of this great man — twenty or more volumes of his autograph letters, personal, public, political, and private; and the girls, with a touch of sentiment mingled with awe, hung over a priceless volume of Franklin's European letters to his wife in America. They were creased and time-stained, but the handwriting was strong and clear, and every letter began " My dear child."

From that hour, as Marian declared, she "just loved Franklin."

There, too, they saw the chair in which Franklin presided at the meetings of his beloved Philosophical Association, when, during his last days, it assembled in his sick-room. Especially did this interest the boys, because of the ingenuity of the wise old man. For the seat of the great chair was reversible : the upper side was a cushioned seat ; the under side, when tipped up, was a ladder by which the sick and aged Franklin could climb into his high four-post bed when the philosophical sessions were over. Uncle Tom declared that this ingenious contrivance impressed the boys mightily, even more than lightning-rods and wise sayings and sidewalks.

At last they sought the final resting-place of this wonderful American, who from a Boston street ballad-seller rose to be the best-known man of his day in the two hemispheres.

Where the high brick fence enclosing the old Christ Church burying-ground has been torn away, at the corner of Arch and Fifth streets, so that all who pass may see the spot from the street, they gathered before the iron railing that separated them from the grave of Franklin.

It was a flat slab lying at their feet, and the girls, still under the influence of the dear home letters they had seen, found a special significance and a peculiar beauty in the simple but joint memorial, inscribed only with the names of Benjamin Franklin and Deborah, his wife.

"His life was just as simple as that slab," said Uncle Tom, as, resting from their wanderings, they sat together beneath the beautiful trees of Independence Square, "and just as eloquent by its very simplicity. And what a life it was! I know of none into which was crowded more of good to the nation and the world, with less of personal ambition or the vanity of glory."

FRANKLIN'S GRAVE.
Fifth and Arch streets, Philadelphia.

"Tell us his story, Uncle Tom," Christine requested. "I sort of know it, but I don't really."

"Briefly, it is this," said Uncle Tom: "A rather harum-scarum boy in the streets of old Boston, he began working on his own hook when twelve years old, selling his own songs through the town, because he did not take kindly to his father's business of candle-making. Then he became a printer, ran away from home to escape the tyranny of a brother, turned up on a Sunday morning here in Philadelphia, and found employment in a printing-office; and here, at twenty years of age, he was patronized by a governor, who sent him to England on false promises. Having a trade, however, he did not starve when failure met him. He returned, after two years in London, to Philadelphia, and set up a printing-office of his own on Market street; he started a newspaper; he became a bookseller, and next an almanac publisher; then he was made clerk of the assembly, postmaster of Philadelphia, and finally postmaster general of the American colonies. A pretty good rise for the candle-maker's son, was it not?"

"I should say it was," said Bert. How old was he when he was made postmaster-general, Uncle Tom?"

"About forty-six," his uncle replied. "But he had accomplished much else. The poor Boston boy, who had scarcely a year's schooling, was now master of six languages. He had tamed the lightning, had made his name known in Europe, received degrees, medals, and diplomas from the leading colleges in Europe and America, and had become, for all time, 'Doctor' Franklin, philosopher and scientist."

"When did he fly the kite that brought him all that fame, Uncle Tom?" asked Marian.

PRINTING PRESS.
IMPOSING STONE.
ELECTRICAL MACHINE
FIRE BUCKETS.
DRESS SWORD.
BUST· BY HOUDON.
COPY OF HEADING OF THE FIRST
NUMBER OF THE PENNSYL-
VANIA GAZETTE PUBLISHED
BY FRANKLIN.
SUGGESTION OF THE OLD PHILA-
DELPHIA LIBRARY IN THE
BACKGROUND.

MEMORIALS OF FRANKLIN.

"On a June day in 1752," Uncle Tom replied, "out here in the fields just beyond the town. Now, of course, that little hill is all built over. I wish I could locate it for you, for it is one of America's historic spots. Well, in 1757 he was sent to England as agent for Pennsylvania, and soon after was made agent, or representative, in England for all the colonies. He stayed there eighteen years, returning in time to be sent to Congress and sign the Declaration of Independence."

"That's the time he made the funny answer to Hancock, was n't it?" said Roger.

"I don't know; what was that, Roger?" Uncle Tom inquired.

"Why, don't you remember? Hancock said, 'We must all be unanimous now; there must be no pulling apart; we must all hang together.' And

A MEETING OF AN OLD-TIME SCIENTIFIC SOCIETY.

Franklin replied, 'That 's true, John; for if we don't, we shall all hang separately.'"

"Cheerful old fellow, was n't he?" said Jack. "I do like a man who can make a joke just when you don't expect it."

"Franklin was always bubbling over with fun," Uncle Tom declared. "The man who was quick to see the deep and serious side of life could also see its sunny and humorous side. That is what helped make him so well rounded. That same year he was sent as minister to the Court of France, and secured the help of that nation for the struggling colonies. He lived there ten years. Then he came home, was made president — that is, governor — of Pennsylvania; went to Congress, and worked for and signed the new Constitution of the United States, when he was eighty-one years old, and, as you know, the oldest signer of that great document. Three years later, on the 17th of April, 1790, he died, aged eighty-four, and now lies buried beside his beloved Deborah, 'his wife,' beneath that simple slab in Christ Church burying-ground."

CHRIST CHURCH, PHILADELPHIA.
Where Franklin and Washington went to church.

"What a busy life!" exclaimed Christine. "And think of the things he did that you could n't get into the story, Uncle Tom! I think he must have been a delightful old man."

"He was indeed, Christine," Uncle Tom replied, "and as remarkable as he was charming. Self-taught, self-reared, self-made, the candle-maker's boy gave light to all the world; the street ballad-seller set all men to singing of liberty; the runaway printer brought the nations to praise and honor him. And he was so well balanced! Witty, but never malicious; inflexible, but never obstinate; strong-willed, but never tyrannical; the wisest of men, but never conceited; a statesman, but never a politician; an office-holder, but never an office-seeker: he had all the attributes and none of the vices of greatness; all the simplicity and none of the sordidness of success. With great understanding, he had still greater common sense, and, while asking few favors for himself, no man in the world ever set on foot so many good works of practical benevolence. Yes, yes; he was a great man, my friends; America's most remarkable production, I contend. Come, let 's go into Independence Hall, and have a look at the Liberty Bell."

WHERE FRANKLIN LIVED IN FRANCE.
Château de Chaumont.

In the center of the very room in which was presented, adopted, and signed the immortal Declaration of Independence, within its protecting case of oak and glass, hung the historic bell which rang out in announcement of the great act of July 4, 1776. The children gathered about it with feelings of the deepest reverence. There, in the side, they saw the crack that burst in it as it tolled for the death of the great Chief-Justice Marshall. About the rim they could read its prophetic inscription: " Proclaim liberty throughout the land unto all the inhabitants thereof"; and Uncle Tom told them that it had been mute and tongueless ever since the one hundred and thirteenth birthday of Washington, when it had struck its last note. But he assured them that, by its silent presence in that memorial hall, and by its carefully guarded journeys north and south to expositions and national jubi-

THE LIBERTY BELL ON A SOUTHERN TRIP.
"Eloquent for loyalty, liberty's most efficient orator."

lees, it had become eloquent for loyalty, liberty's most efficient orator. Even more than the table on which the Declaration had been signed and the chairs in which had sat the members of the Congress, did this voiceless old bell hold and fascinate the boys and girls.

Uncle Tom shared their interest.

"It certainly is one of the most impressive relics in the world," he declared, as they passed from the Congress room to the National Museum across the hall. "I always feel as though I were looking on a real participator in the historic event which it proclaimed so vigorously a hundred years or more ago."

"As you are," Bert declared; while Christine, looking at the winding hall stair, exclaimed :

"Oh, was it up those stairs that the boy ran to tell his grandfather to ring ? "

"You remember the old story, do you ? " laughed Uncle Tom. "Those should be the stairs, if they have not been renewed or rebuilt. As to the truth of that story, I am not prepared to decide."

"It 's good enough to be true, anyhow," said Roger.

"It 's all just like the poem," said Christine. "Let 's see, how did it go ? " and she repeated the opening verse of the bell-ringer story as she had spoken it in school :

JULY 4, 1776.

"Squarely prim and stoutly built,
Free from glitter and from gilt,
Plain, from lintel up to roof-tree and to belfry
    bare and brown,
Stands the Hall that hot July,
While the folk throng anxious by,
Where the Continental Congress meets within
    the Quaker town.

"Hark! a stir, a sudden shout,
And a boy comes springing out,
Signalling to where his grandsire in the
    belfry waiting stands:
'Ring!' he cries; 'the deed is done!
Ring! they 've signed, and freedom 's
    won!'
And the ringer grasps the bell-rope with his
    strong and sturdy hands;
While the Bell, with joyous note,
Clanging from its brazen throat,
Rings the tidings, all-exultant — peals the
    news from shore to sea:
'*Man is man — a slave no longer.
Truth and Right than Might are stronger.
Praise to God! we 're free; we 're free!*'"

They lingered long over the extensive collection of revolutionary relics in the museum room; they visited the Congress Hall, where Washington and Adams had both been inaugurated; they hunted up the Supreme Court room in which had presided John Jay and Oliver Ellsworth, earliest of chief-justices. They studied or recalled all the associations that make Independence Hall so notable an object lesson in American history, and Marian stood before the ancient fireplace in the Philosophical rooms on the exact spot where Washington posed for the celebrated Gilbert Stuart portrait.

"Gilbert Stuart!" said Bert, "O, don't you remember? we found his grave in Boston."

"Yes, in the old burying ground, inside of Boston Common," replied Roger.

TABLE AND CHAIRS USED AT THE SIGNING OF
THE DECLARATION.

They visited Carpenters' Hall, farther down Chestnut street — a quaint reminder of colonial times, hedged about by great modern buildings, but with tiny courtyard and grass-plots. They read the inscription above the doors of the audience room: "Within these walls, Henry, Hancock, and Adams inspired the delegates of the colonies with nerve and sinew for the toils of war," and then were quite ready to hunt up that historic corner of Seventh and Market streets where, so the tablet in the new bank building announced to them, had stood the house in which Jefferson wrote the Declaration.

PORTRAIT OF WILLIAM PENN, IN HIS TWENTY-SECOND YEAR.

They dipped still deeper into the past, and hunted up the site of the old houses which William Penn, the founder of Pennsylvania, had built for himself and his daughter on Letitia street, and so, at last, worked round again to dinner and the contemplation of Franklin — Philadelphia's most notable figure, as Uncle Tom declared.

"I told you in Boston," he remarked, as the hungry tourists paused awhile between the roast and the dessert, "that, looking upon the spot where Franklin was born, I was inclined to put him down as the first real American. The study of his life here in this city, for which he did so much, only strengthens me in that opinion. Benjamin Franklin was the product of his own age and the child of his own country."

"How could he have been anything else," remarked practical Jack.

"It does sound a bit like a self-evident truth, Jack, I admit," laughed Uncle Tom. "But I hope you know what I mean. He was preëminently what is called the 'child of his age' because he did more than any other

American to glorify his age and shape the destinies of his country. The ballad-peddler of Boston, the runaway printer's apprentice, made his name famous in two continents, and, for his native land, joined liberty and law to progress and common sense. Here, in this fine old city, he organized education, benevolence, and industry; here he conquered the lightning, established independence, and cemented union. With Franklin as a model, our boys can aspire to anything and accomplish much. With his life as a guide and his integrity as a text, the American of to-day can shape himself into a better patriot, a broader-minded American, a more devoted citizen of the republic. Now for Fairmount Park and the charming Wissahickon!"

BIRD'S-EYE VIEW OF PHILADELPHIA FROM CAMDEN, N. J.
Delaware River in foreground.

A LANDING ON THE CHESAPEAKE.

Leonard Calvert at St. Mary's, 1634

FROM THE PAINTING BY HENRY SANDHAM

CHAPTER VI

AT THE GATEWAY OF THE WEST

Philadelphia's Place in History — A New Plan of Pilgrimage — In the Mouth of the Chesapeake — The Old Dominion — Richmond and Patrick Henry.

"*ENI, Vidi, Vici!*" exclaimed Bert, as, their three days' stay in Philadelphia over, the boys and girls were on their way back to New York.

"Modest, even for a classical crank!" retorted Jack. "How have you conquered, Mr. Julius Cæsar Albert Upham?"

"Why, I mean we 've seen about everything there is to see in our line in Philadelphia," exclaimed Bert. "Is n't that so?"

"Right you are," replied Jack, "and I 'm bound to confess, Roger my boy," he added, turning to his Boston friend, "that, historically at least, the Quaker City pushes the Hub pretty close. I had n't any idea, Uncle Tom, that Philadelphia was such a treasure chest of relics."

"Live and learn, Jack," said Uncle Tom. "The fact is, scarcely any city in the United States possesses so many historic buildings and sites as Philadelphia. It is one of the oldest municipalities, and has kept steadily advancing since Penn's day. For years it was the national capital, and it has been its good fortune to have carefully and watchfully preserved many of the buildings that have a place in American history."

They had scoured the old city thoroughly, from Penn's landing-place and Franklin's "cake walk," as Jack insisted on calling lower Market street, to the new City Hall and Grant's "headquarters" cottage in Fairmount Park. They saw a game of ball at Girard College; went through the splendid new bourse,— the "home of the money-changers," Uncle Tom called it; visited the Zoo and the Memorial Art Building, reminders of the nation's one hundredth birthday; saw Decatur's grave in the old burying-ground

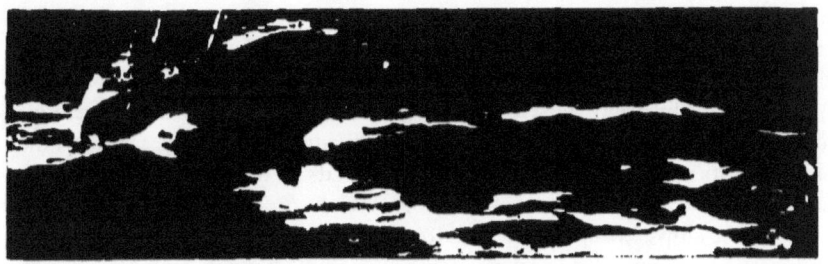

THE INVESTIGATORS SOUTHWARD BOUND.

on Third street; and even extended their investigations to Germantown and Valley Forge.

Now they were homeward bound; but Uncle Tom had not yet reached the end. He had a new plan to propose; and when, after a few days at home, he brought it to the attention of what Marian called his "pilgrim band," it was, naturally, greeted with shouts of approval.

This new plan was nothing more than a trip by water to Fort Monroe, and then, striking inland, a spring excursion to the homes of certain great and famous Americans.

Uncle Tom's plan was warmly assented to by Mr. Dunlap, the father of Jack and Marian. For, as you may remember, when he first sent them to Washington to study the Government under Uncle Tom's direction, Mr. Dunlap had insisted that young Americans should see and know their own land first before attempting Europe.

It so happened that the homes of the great men " slated" by Uncle Tom all lay on or near a direct route to the West. It did not "happen," however, Uncle Tom assured them. "Nothing happens," he said. "There is a reason for all things." And it was with reason, he declared, that nearly all America's famous ones were "border" men, and, hence, that western lay their line of travel. Once decided upon, the energetic "personal conductor" soon had the trip planned, the excursion tickets procured, all minor details arranged, and within four days after decision the five tourists and their mentor were at sea, southward bound.

It was early in the morning when the steamer passed the lonely light-ship off Cape Charles and entered Chesapeake Bay. Even there the broad gateway to the West looked like the open sea; but Uncle Tom reminded the boys and girls of the historic events that wide waterway had witnessed since first Spaniard and Frenchman tacked cautiously in, searching for the "Western Passage" to Cathay in the early days of American discovery.

"Here, sailing into fame," said Uncle Tom, sweeping with his comprehensive gesture the water-line that stretched from cape to cape, "came Captain John Smith, most adventurous of Englishmen; over this course came the early Virginia colonists, and, later, Lord Delaware and the founder of Maryland. Out from here, bound for their English home, sailed Pocahontas and John Rolfe; and in between these sandy shores came the famous Dutch ship with its cargo of negro slaves and the seeds of future discord. Pioneers and pirates, traders and travelers, Roundheads and Cavaliers, supply ships and prison ships, troop ships and tobacco ships, royal governors, arrogant and assuming, royal governors, disgusted or disgraced — all these, in the early days, sailed in or out through this broad water-gate, to the help or the hindrance of the Old Dominion and the future republic."

"Why was it called the Old Dominion, Uncle Tom?" Bert inquired.

"Virginia so styled herself because of her steadfast loyalty to the good-for-nothing Stuarts all through the days of the English Commonwealth and the mighty Cromwell," Uncle Tom replied, with the emphasis to be expected of so sturdy an ad-

"HERE THEY SAILED INTO FAME."

mirer of Cromwell, so firm a hater of the Stuarts. Indeed, Uncle Tom impressed it upon his tourists that America would never sufficiently honor herself until in the capital of the republic should rise a statue of the man to whom America owes so much — Oliver Cromwell, greatest of Englishmen.

"The Stuarts have their trade-marks all about this region," Uncle Tom declared. "These two capes between which we are passing were named for the two Stuart boys — Henry and Charles, sons of that crowned blockhead of a James who so scandalously put to death the father of Virginia and one of the beginners of American history and progress, Sir Walter Raleigh, soldier and statesman."

"Oh, he was the cloak-man, was n't he?" cried Marian. "I mean the young courtier who spread his velvet mantle in the mud for Queen Elizabeth to walk over."

"That was Raleigh," assented Uncle Tom; "and though he never sailed these waters himself, he sent expeditions here, and did much toward the establishment of Virginia and the development of America. A noble historic figure is Raleigh, boys and girls. You should know his story, both for its dramatic outlines and for the bearing it has on American history."

The steamer plowed its steady course through this gleaming water-gate to the West, while Uncle Tom, still intent on giving a real atmosphere to facts, continued his catalogue of happenings that had made their surroundings historic.

"Over these shining waters and past these low-lying shores," he said, "sped the messenger bearing to the worthless Charles Stuart, known as Charles the Second,

RALEIGH AND ELIZABETH.

and then a fugitive in Flanders, the colony's invitation to come to the Old Dominion and be crowned King of Virginia. Here sailed the Virginia vessels that were a part of that ill-fated expedition against Carthagena in South America, led by the English admiral Vernon, who gave his name to the dearly loved Potomac home of Washington — Mount Vernon. Here sailed George Washington himself on the only foreign 'tour' he ever attempted, when, as a boy of eighteen, he accompanied his sick brother Lawrence to Barbadoes. Here, years after, came the ships of the Frenchman De Grasse, sailing to the final victory of the Revolution at Yorktown — that way, to the north; and here, eighty years later, Northern and Southern seamen met in fight on that momentous March day in 1862, when a certain little 'cheese-box on a raft' — the plucky *Monitor* — came steaming along right where we are now, and, just in the nick of time, put an

WHEN THE SUPPLY SHIP CAME IN, IN OLD VIRGINIA DAYS.

BIRD'S-EYE VIEW OF THE BATTLE BETWEEN THE "MONITOR" AND THE "MERRIMAC."

end to destruction, and revolutionized the naval war-fare of the world. See, before us lies Hampton Roads!"

The great sheet of water stretched on before them, shining in the bright spring sun. To the right rose the green sloping battlements of Fort Monroe, backed by the great hotels of Old Point Comfort; to the left lay the wooded Virginia shores; far ahead, the broad channel showed the way to Norfolk city, broken only by the odd little island of the Rip Raps, with its dis-mantled fort, between which and the yellow beach of Old Point Comfort they saw swinging at anchor the great white water-birds of the new American navy.

"The heirs, executors, and assigns of the little *Monitor*, eh, Uncle Tom?" said Bert.

"And right here was where the fight came off, was it?" cried Jack, while the girls capped his query with the verdict, "How interesting!"

"Yes; there, before us, lies the scene of that now famous encounter," Uncle Tom replied — "the only incident of the Civil War, by the way," he continued, "that Congress allows a place on the walls of the Capitol. There you saw, when you were in Wash-ington, you remember, the picture of the fight be-tween the *Merrimac* and the *Monitor;* not because it was a Northern victory,— for, indeed, it was really but a drawn battle,— but because that memorable sea-fight marked a new era in naval history, and made a new starting-point for the navies of the world. Just now, gentlemen and ladies, you are sailing over an historic point. For here was the beginning of the formidable modern navy, in which yonder great White Squadron has so prominent a place."

"Mighty interesting piece of water this, is n't it?" said Jack, voicing the general opinion of the "crowd."

But Roger, with thoughts of Plymouth Rock and Fort Warren in mind, was inclined to enter a quali-fication.

"That 's only because Uncle Tom makes it so,"

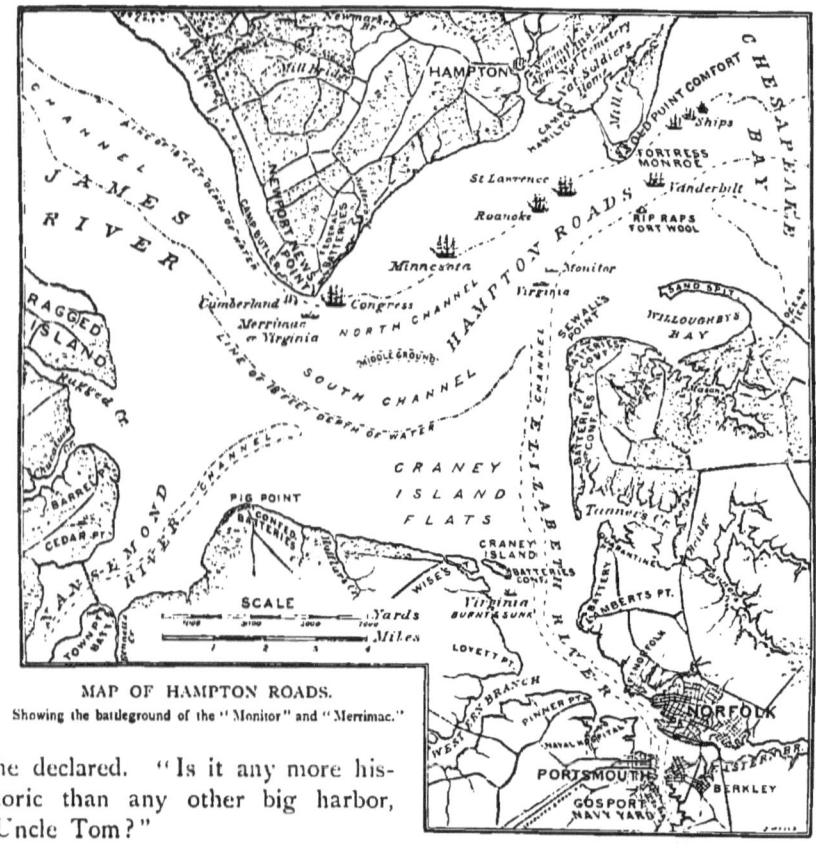

MAP OF HAMPTON ROADS.
Showing the battleground of the "Monitor" and "Merrimac."

he declared. "Is it any more historic than any other big harbor, Uncle Tom?"

"Not any more so, but fully as historic, Roger," Uncle Tom replied. "In fact, the great bays on our Atlantic coast-line have all been, since discovery, gateways to the West, and through their open portals have ceaselessly come the makers of America—peculiar people all. Into Massachusetts Bay sailed Pilgrim and Puritan; into New York Bay, Dutchman and Walloon; into Delaware Bay, Swede and Quaker; into Chesapeake Bay, Cavalier, Churchman, and Catholic; and into the Carolina sounds, Scotchman and German. All of these, in their way, made each great water-gate historic, as through privation and pluck they became colonists, Englishmen, Americans. But at first the elements were all singularly diverse. We need to remember, when we grumble about foreign immigration, that we were all foreigners once; that the red Indian is the only native American, and that we attained our birthright gradually and by slow development."

THE "MONITOR" AND THE "MERRIMAC."

"But surely, Uncle Tom," exclaimed dainty Marian, "you would n't put our ancestors alongside the riffraff that comes in the steerage to-day, would you?"

But for answer Uncle Tom, too wise to be led into argument, merely turned to his niece with a smile, and dropped into poetry.

"'T is distance lends enchantment to the view,
And robes the mountain in its azure hue,"

he said. "Come! all off for Old Point! To-day we are the immigrants."

A delightful day was spent on that sandy spot where, of old, the storm-tossed Virginia colonists first found relief and solid ground, and gratefully called the land Point Comfort.

The young people critically examined the two great hotels, they visited the White Squadron, they roamed about the green embrasured fortress that fronts the sea and gives a martial air to the little town that has grown up about it. The boys studied the preparations for mounting the queer new "disappearing gun," the girls walked the whole circuit of the wide, water-filled moat, and felt almost like medieval maidens in some moated castle of the days of Ivanhoe or Quentin Durward, while all the young people gazed with equal interest upon the room that had been Jefferson Davis's prison,

THE NATIVE AND THE IMMIGRANT.
A struggle for possession in the early days of America.

and the grove of live oaks on the great parade-
ground, beneath which the boys and girls who have
the delightful experience of living inside a fortress
were bicycling or playing ball.

After a most interesting trolley-trip to Hampton
and its famous school,— fit monument to the vigor,
patience, and self-sacrifice of that true American,
General Armstrong,— the whole party boarded the

"THE GREEN EMBRASURED
FORTRESS THAT FRONTS THE SEA."

train, backed all the way down
to Newport News, and then
steamed "on to Richmond,"
eighty miles away. The road
lay through a region rich in
the associations of two stirring
epochs in American history —
the Revolution and the Civil
War.

"Over that way, a few miles to the east." Uncle Tom said, "lies Yorktown, where the Revolution came to an end, while here to the right, at our
very next stopping-place, was sounded one of the first bugle-blasts of the
Revolution."

"What place is that?" queried Marian.

But Bert was already studying his time-table.

"Williamsburg," he announced.   "Let 's see; is n't there an old, old
college there?"

"Yes," Uncle Tom replied; "William and Mary College, the oldest
college in the United States, excepting Harvard.   Washington was its chan-
cellor; Presidents Jefferson, Monroe, and Tyler, Chief-Justice Marshall, and
General Winfield Scott were once students there.   In that old town were
the headquarters of Nathaniel Bacon, earliest of American rebels against

kingly authority. There stood the old Capitol building in which Washington sat as a burgess, and in which young Thomas Jefferson heard Patrick Henry's first famous and fiery speech against the crown."

"That was n't the 'liberty-or-death' speech, was it, Uncle Tom?" asked Roger.

"No; it was earlier than that," Uncle Tom replied. "It was the speech he made in connection with his resolutions against the Stamp Act, and in it

THE PRINCIPAL STREET OF YORKTOWN.

he thundered out: 'Cæsar had his Brutus, Charles the First his Cromwell, and George the Third—' 'Treason, treason!' came the cry from the scandalized loyalists,— 'may profit by their example,' said Henry; and then added, 'If this be treason, make the most of it!'"

"That was great!" cried Jack. "I tell you, he had sand, had n't he!"

"How that must have rattled those old Tories!" said Roger.

NATHANIEL BACON.
"Earliest of American rebels against kingly authority."

"It did n't rattle Mr. P. Henry, though, did it?" said Jack.   "A great orator, was n't he, Uncle Tom?"

"Did he ever do anything more than that speech and the 'liberty-or-death' one?" inquired Marian.

"Who? Henry? Why," said Uncle Tom, "he was for years one of the foremost figures in Virginia history. We remember him to-day only for those two famous speeches, but he filled many offices, declined many, and just escaped election as Vice-President."

"Then he must have had a story, the same as the other men you have told us about," said Christine. "Did n't he, Uncle Tom?"

"Yes, my dear; he had a story," Uncle Tom replied. "He began with the same unpromising youth so many great men have shown. He was a careless country boy, loving hunting and fishing more than study, loafing more than books—"

"Who does n't?" said Jack, *sotto voce*. But Uncle Tom heard him.

"Not you, Jack, I 'm sure," he said.

"What! think I had n't rather go fishing than peg away at problems in geometry?" cried Jack. "Well, I guess!"

"Now, Jack, I 'm not going to think as poorly of you as that," protested Uncle Tom. "Of course I 'll admit that a shady bank, a hook and line, and plenty of bites are more interesting than a proposition in Euclid; but as between the two for a real mind developer and intellectual spur, I don't think so practical and wide-awake a fellow as you would hesitate in choice. Greatness comes because of persistence quite as much as because of genius, and it was persistence even more than genius that made our dozen or more famous Americans great and immortal."

PATRICK HENRY.

"But about Patrick Henry," prompted Bert, who always liked to stick to the subject.

"Did n't he have genius?" asked Jack.

"I should not call it genius," said Uncle Tom. "With him it was more the inspiration of the moment or the spur of necessity that turned his tongue to fire. He was what we might call an instigator to liberty, as was Otis in Boston, and the boy Hamilton in New York."

"How soon was it before he became an orator?" Marian inquired.

"Not until he was twenty-seven years old," was Uncle Tom's reply. "His youth, as I have told you, was a careless, happy-go-lucky existence; he never succeeded at anything and stuck to nothing long. But when at last he blundered into eloquence, under a terrible pressure,— in what is known in history as 'the Parsons' cause,' a matter of church taxes which the people resisted,— he sprang at once into popularity as 'the people's champion.'"

"That, I suppose, set him up in business," suggested Jack.

"It certainly did," said Uncle Tom. "From that day he became a prominent figure in Virginia history. It brought him practice as a lawyer, advancement as a public man, power as a politician. He became a member of the House of Burgesses,— what we call the legislature, you know,— a political leader in Virginia, a delegate to the first and second Continental Congresses, first commander of Virginia's Revolutionary army, first governor of the State of Virginia, being twice reëlected. After that, he declined to serve as member of the Constitutional Convention, as United States senator, as secretary of State, as governor of Virginia for the fourth time, as Chief-Justice of the United States, as ambassador to France, and as Vice-President of the United States. One or all of these high honors might have been Patrick Henry's had he but said yes."

"Well, I don't see but he had a fine record as a decliner," said Roger.

"Must have gone into a decline early," suggested Jack the incorrigible.

"Many a true word is spoken in jest, boy Jack," Uncle Tom said with a smile. "That really was a leading reason for those continued refusals to hold office. For the last twenty-five years of his life Henry was a confirmed invalid, and, as you grow older, boys and girls, you will learn that ill health dulls the edge of energy."

"I suppose it does take the starch out of a fellow," said Jack. "But seems to me our 'liberty-or-death' friend might have braced up and stuck to things."

"Well, I suppose he would have done so had he been better satisfied with the way things were going," Uncle Tom replied. "But, you see, there was a lot of criticism afloat in those early days of the republic, and that was one thing that Parick Henry could not stand. He hated to have his motives questioned, and he chafed under restraint. That, in fact, was one cause of his eloquence. As an orator he had remarkable powers; but as a leader he was uncertain and a bit headstrong, so that he often found his boat in troubled waters."

"But Washington trusted him," asserted Bert.

"Yes; Washington saw his good points and appreciated his sincerity, devotion, and loyalty," Uncle Tom replied. "Washington could handle him, and it is certainly to the credit of Patrick Henry that two such wise and well-balanced men as Washington and Adams stood his friends and defenders."

WASHINGTON, PATRICK HENRY, AND EDMUND PENDLETON,
On their way to Philadelphia as delegates to the First Continental Congress

Their study of Patrick Henry's character was resumed when, next day, they, as Jack expressed it, "crossed his tracks again" in Richmond.

It was in the old church of St. John, a plain but picturesque old bit of pre-Revolutionary architecture, standing on Church Hill, on the corner of Broadway and Twenty-fourth streets. A trolley car left them at the gate. Christine declared she never could get used to the strange mixture of the old and the new—"trolley cars and Patrick Henry!" she exclaimed.

The sexton came from his little office building and unlocked the side door of the old church, which, he explained, had been considerably enlarged since Revolutionary days.

"It must have been a bandbox then," was Marian's comment, "for it is n't very big now."

But large or small, it was big with interest for them all. For when the sexton, pointing to the third pew in the little block of seats on the right of

7

the entrance, informed them that "in that pew Patrick Henry made his great speech that every boy and girl of you knows by heart, I reckon." there was an immediate scramble by the five to stand on the identical spot where the familiar words were uttered.

Jack, indeed, with his irrepressible spirits, faced the chancel where the chairman of the convention sat on that memorable March day in 1775, and would at once have branched out into the famous speech.

But when he had gone as far as " Mr. President, it is natural to man to indulge in the illusions of hope," Uncle Tom interfered, and reminded him that oratory was not included in the permission to enter.

The pleas of the other boys and girls, however, who always liked to hear Jack "orate," and the good nature of the interested

THE OLD CHURCH OF ST. JOHN, RICHMOND.

sexton, led Uncle Tom to compromise on the closing paragraph of the oration, which Jack rendered with appreciation and effect, standing in the precise spot from which those wonderful words were uttered by Patrick Henry a hundred and twenty years and more ago:

"It is in vain, sir, to extenuate the matter. Gentlemen may cry peace, peace, but there is no peace. The war is actually begun. The next gale that sweeps from the north will bring to our ears the clash of resounding arms. Our brethren are already in the field. Why stand we here idle? What is it that gentlemen wish? What would they have? Is life so dear or peace so sweet as to be purchased at the price of chains and slavery? Forbid it, Almighty God! I know not what course others may take, but as for me, give me liberty, or give me death!"

"That was a great speech, was n't it, though!" Roger remarked, as, leaving the church, they stood in the shade of one of the spreading trees, trying to decipher the inscription on an ancient stone. "I don't wonder it has never been forgotten."

"It was never forgotten by those who heard it, friend or foe," Uncle

INTERIOR OF ST. JOHN'S CHURCH, RICHMOND.

Patrick Henry made his famous speech standing in the pew on the left, near the door, marked by a tablet.

"I HAVE HEARD BOYS IN SCHOOL
TEAR IT INTO TATTERS"

Tom declared. "No report was made of it at the time, but, until old age, men who had listened to it in breathless excitement could recall its burning sentences and the method of delivery. Jack gave the close very well. I have heard boys in school tear it into tatters when they came to the 'liberty or death.' But that was not Patrick Henry's style of oratory. There is to-day in the library of Cornell University a manuscript account of the speech, written by one who heard and never forgot it. This is the way, according to the writer, that Patrick Henry gave the closing sentence: 'Is life so dear or peace so sweet as to be purchased at the price of chains and slavery?' he uttered in the attitude of one condemned to slavery, bowed under the weight of fetters. With that he paused, and raising hand and eyes to heaven, prayed, 'Forbid it, Almighty God!' Dropping his hand, he turned toward the Tories and Loyalists, who sat spell-bound and terrified at his audacious speech, and with form bent low he said hopelessly, 'I know not what course others may take,' and then, straightening himself as if straining against his fetters, he hissed through clenched teeth, 'but as for me,' changing into the triumphant trumpet call, 'give me liberty;' thus he stood, as the manuscript says, 'a magnificent incarnation of Freedom,' until, finally, after an impressive pause, his left hand dropped to his side powerless; his right hand was clenched, as if holding a dagger to his breast; then it struck the imaginary weapon into his heart as the closing words came out, fearlessly, victoriously, like a heroic dirge — 'or give me death!' There you have the methods of a born orator, boys and girls. I 'm afraid if you tried it that way, however, you might overdo the thing; for it is but a step, you know, from the sublime to the ridiculous. But Patrick Henry was an orator above everything else; and it is as the orator of resistance, of liberty, of patriotism that America will remember him forever and ever."

"Where did he live, Uncle Tom? Here in Richmond?" Christine inquired, still interested in the search for "local color."

"No, not in Richmond," Uncle Tom replied. "Henry lived quite a way to the southwest of Richmond, in what is now Charlotte County, just a few miles south of historic Appomattox. His fine plantation was called Red Hill, and to-day it is the country residence of the great orator's descendants, to one of whom I hope to introduce you all to-day."

This was interesting, and, in fact, Uncle Tom did keep his promise. For, later in the day, each one of the five was presented to a courteous and delightful "gentleman of the old school" whom they afterward referred to as "the real grandson of the real Patrick Henry."

The incident impressed them strongly, for they felt as if, somehow, they had been brought by that introduction into direct contact with that great and glorious past which had proclaimed liberty to the nations and given a new and splendid republic to the world.

A FAMOUS RICHMOND MAN.

John Marshall, Chief Justice of the United States.

CHAPTER VII

A FAMOUS OLD CAPITAL

Richmond on the James — A City Set on a Hill — Relics and Reminders — A Jeffersonian Atmosphere — No Sectionalism in Heroism.

HE young people were delighted with Richmond. As, early in the morning, the best time to see any place to advantage, they rode about the famous old capital from one historic point to another, they were quite ready to echo Daniel Webster's verdict, " Truly, the city hath a pleasant seat."

"Daniel Webster?" exclaimed Bert. " Why, I thought that was Shakspere — in ' Macbeth.' "

"Quite right, Mr. Scholar," replied Uncle Tom, who had made the quotation ; " only Shakspere says ' castle,' you know, and Daniel Webster had a way of making pat applications of familiar quotations. And it applied here, don't you think ? "

" I should say it did," returned Bert, who seemed specially impressed with the commanding position of the city. " Why," he continued, " I had no idea Richmond was so high up. No wonder it took our soldiers four years to get it. I 'll bet if the South had been as well fixed as we were in men and supplies it would have taken us four times four years to get in here."

Jack was inclined to dissent from this opinion.

"Not with Grant to lead," he exclaimed. " He 'd have hammered it down in no time, no matter how many forts it had ; would n't he, Uncle Tom ? "

But Uncle Tom was not to be drawn into any such argument.

"Well, you see it was n't a question of ' if,' boys," he replied. " It was a hard enough job to take Richmond just as it was. And — the war 's over ! But, as Bert says, the position of the city makes Richmond, when well protected, almost impregnable. Its situation is certainly a commanding one.

Set on these hills like a coronet, it looks abroad over the land and, indeed, like the city in the Bible, "cannot be hid.'"

"And just see the James winding down there among the woods and fields!" cried Marian. "Is n't it perfectly charming? Was n't it near here somewhere, Uncle Tom, that Pocahontas lived?"

"Yes; ten or twelve miles down the river," her uncle replied, "in, the great loop of lowland about which the river winds, and which has the queer name of Dutch Gap. Look down there, girls, and romance to your hearts' content; for in that valley of the James our most famous love-story came true."

Christine, looking down toward the home of Pocahontas, recalled her Thackeray, and said half aloud:

"Who will shield the fearless heart?
    Who avert the murd'rous blade?
From the throng, with sudden start,
    See! there springs an Indian maid.
Quick she stands before the knight,
    ' Loose the chain, unbind the ring;
    I am daughter of the king
And I claim the Indian right!'

"Dauntlessly aside she flings
    Lifted ax and thirsty knife;
Fondly to his heart she clings,
    And her bosom guards his life!
In the woods of Powhattan,
    Still 'tis told by Indian fires
    How a daughter of their sires
Saved the captive Englishman."

"Pocahontas did save Smith, did n't she, Uncle Tom? I just won't believe what the books say now," Marian declared.

"Why was n't it Rolfe she saved?" queried Christine. "Then the romance would have been completed."

Matoaks als Rebecka daughter to the mighty Prince Powhatan Emperour of Attanoughskomouck als virginia converted and baptized in the Christian faith, and wife to the worp. Mr. Joh Rolff.

POCAHONTAS.

From the engraving in the first edition of John Smith's General History.

But the boys, alive to the life of to-day, rather than the romance of a misty past, were looking down upon the city at their feet.

The carriages had halted on the crest of Libby Hill, at the eastern end of the town, and, close beside the tall shaft of the soldiers' monument, the sight-seers were "drinking in the view."

"It 's a much bigger and busier place than I expected to see," Roger declared.

"It is New Richmond you 're looking at, Roger," Uncle Tom replied. "Many things, you see, have happened since Daniel Webster's Shaksperian verdict. Richmond has made great strides even since I saw it last. Broad streets, fine residences, electric lights, trolley cars, that splendid new hotel, big business blocks — all these indicate a prosperity in which every American will rejoice. For, you see, Richmond is one of our show towns, with a past that is historic."

JOHN SMITH.
From the engraving on Smith's Map of Virginia.

"Let 's hunt it down, then, Uncle Tom," said Jack. "Drive on, please. I want to see Hollywood."

They saw Hollywood — that beautiful city of the dead, with its ruined portal masked in living green. They stood beside the scarcely picturesque "iron summer-house sort of canopy," as Roger styled it, that marks the resting-place of President Monroe; they stood above the unmarked grave of President Tyler; they saw the ivy-covered pyramid of stone that rises as a memorial to thousands of Confederate dead; they saw the graves of Pickett, Hill, and Stuart, famous rebel fighters in the stirring days of '61; they heard the story of other notable names, and then they rode back to town and the things of to-day.

But in Richmond the things of to-day touch elbows with the things of yesterday — and the day before.

"Richmond is the Boston of the South for historic associations," Uncle Tom declared, searching for a comparison that his young people would appreciate. "Its story reaches back to 1609 and John Smith. It knew Pocahontas and Powhatan. Here gallant Nat Bacon flung out his standard of rebellion against the king's governor; from here went the first shipments of tobacco and the first sentiments of revolution. Here Patrick Henry spoke for liberty, and Arnold, the traitor, brought fire and sword; here the rebellious South set up its banner and established its capital, and here was the central stage on which 'the Lost Cause' played its brief but bloody part. A city of relics and reminders is this, with a story stretching from Nathaniel Bacon to Jefferson Davis, and from Thomas Jefferson to ——"

"The hotel!" put in Bert. Whew! There's democratic simplicity for you, eh, Uncle Tom? What do you suppose Jefferson would say, if his statue should come to life in those gorgeous surroundings?"

"That's so; what would he? He was the man who tied his horse to the fence rail and just went in to be inaugurated, was n't he?" said Jack. "Seems to me, Uncle Tom, we run up against the Father of the Declaration wherever we go."

"That's natural, Jack," said Uncle Tom. "Jefferson is in the air here." "Is that so? Smells to me like tobacco," said Jack, with a critical sniff.

They all laughed, and Uncle Tom accepted Jack's amendment. "So far as tangible smells are concerned, you are right," he said. "That build-

"WHAT NEWS? WHAT NEWS?"
In "gallant Nat Bacon's" day.

ing to the left is one of the largest tobacco factories in the world, and the fragrant weed ——"

"Fragrant? Oh, Uncle Tom!" cried Marian.

"I speak in a general sense, my dear," said her uncle, "and as a prevalent, unconfined perfume, I must say it is—well—a bit fragrant. And here in Richmond it is a chief staple, for it gives steady employment to thousands of workers, and does a yearly business of millions of dollars."

"And all to go up in smoke," persisted Marian, who, you see, had her opinions. "What a waste!"

"Nothing is a waste that is productive, my dear," said Uncle Tom. "And really, you know, tobacco has played an important part in the history of this country."

"To be sure," said Bert. "It gave Washington his fortune, so that he would n't take a cent for what he did in the Revolution."

AN IMPORTANT PERSONAGE OF COLONIAL DAYS.
The captain of a train-band.

"And Grant won his victories on it," said Jack.

But still Marian was not convinced, and the talk might have drifted into a discussion of the tobacco habit if Uncle Tom had not drawn it back to the original topic.

"The personal atmosphere," he declared, "is Jefferson. He, as I said, is in the air. You feel his presence growing upon you gradually all the way up from Williamsburg. There he went to college; there he made his first entry into public life; here he won position and fame. The fine old Capitol yonder was designed by him; here he served three terms as governor of his State in a rough and stormy time, and, all about, you find traces or reminders of this remarkable man. For fifty years Thomas Jefferson was Virginia's representative man."

"Jefferson!" exclaimed Roger. "What 's the matter with Washington?"

"He 's — all — right!" Jack vociferated, and Uncle Tom added:

"Washington, Roger, was America's representative man."

"Well, that 's so, of course," Roger admitted. "But was n't Jefferson, too?"

"Assuredly, to a certain extent," Uncle Tom replied. "But this section of the Old Dominion was especially his. Washington was never here very much. We do not 'cross his tracks,' as Jack puts it, so often here as we shall in the Potomac region, where he lived as boy and man.   But Jefferson was three times governor of Virginia ; he framed Virginia's constitution, and built himself into the State in many ways.   No wonder, then, that he and Patrick Henry stand on the base of that splendid Washington monument

yonder in Capitol Park, and that his heroic figure graces the grand new hotel that has been honored with his name.   So, you see, in this section Jefferson is the man for us to study rather than Washington, who will claim our attention later in our tour."

They dismissed their carriage at the hotel, and spent the rest of that day and a good part of the next, in cars or on foot, visiting the points of interest to which they wished to devote time for careful inspection.

The list of such places was a long one.

They visited the notable monuments in the city, from Crawford's Washington in Capitol Park to Lee on horseback at the farther end of Franklin Street.   They saw the famous Washington, by Houdon, the Frenchman — esteemed the best of all statues of Washington, because modeled from life; they viewed the Stonewall Jackson monument, near the governor's house;

HOUDON'S STATUE OF WASHINGTON.
In the State Capitol, Richmond.

they inspected the old Capitol, designed by Jefferson, and in which the Confederate congress held its sessions during that stirring time of war, from 1861 to 1865.

This old capitol building was especially productive of explanation and discussion ; but the things in it by which the boys and girls were most impressed were the rusty old picture depicting the storming a redoubt at Yorktown — "Perhaps the very charge," suggested Roger, "in which Alexander Hamilton ended the Revolution," — and those two Colonial antiques, the Speaker's chair of the old House of Burgesses, and the funny three-storied stove in the Rotunda Gallery.

In that very chair, Christine, who, the boys declared, "never weakened on Washington," was positive, the Speaker must have sat when he said to

Washington, who had "stage fright" when he tried to reply to the Colony's vote of thanks for driving the French out of Fort Duquesne: "Sit down, Mr. Washington. Your modesty equals your valor, and that surpasses the power of any language I possess."

"Oh, what a pretty compliment!" cried Marian. "Who said it, Christine?"

"The Speaker of the House of Burgesses at Williamsburg," replied Christine. "I don't know his name; do you, Uncle Tom?"

"He was Mr. Robinson," Uncle Tom answered; "and, as Christine says, it is very probable that he was sitting in this very chair when he made Washington blush."

"Well, I think this old stove is simply cute," Marian declared. "I can just imagine Jefferson warming his hands before it."

"Or Patrick Henry turning from it to say, 'We must fight,' and so warming up the whole country to action," declared Bert.

"Very neatly put, Bert," Uncle Tom declared, with a nod of approval, "even if it is a question whether those hardy Virginia farmers would have a fire going in this elegant affair in the spring. Come, let us go across to the State Library and see the portraits."

They spent an hour in that treasure-house of Colonial, Revolutionary and Civil War times, the State Library; then, passing around Capitol Square, they located the various State offices of the defunct Confederacy, had a look at the governor's mansion in the park, and visited the "White House of the Confederacy"—the house in which Jefferson Davis had lived during the war. They saw the house of Chief-Justice Marshall, now old and time-worn. They saw on Main street the roomy old Allan mansion, in which Edgar Allan Poe lived as a boy. They stood, as you already know, in the very pew in old St. John's Church from which Patrick Henry

OLD STOVE IN STATE CAPITOL.

declared for liberty or death; they saw that later church, with the needle-like spire, where Davis received word from Lee that the cause was lost and Richmond must be evacuated; they visited the "Monumental Church," erected on the site of the dreadful Richmond theater fire of 1811; they admired Richmond College standing in its attractive grounds near to the Lee monument; they located, as far as possible, the notable battle spots

RICHMOND IN 1861.

within range of Richmond, the site of Libby Prison, the old Slave Market, Belle Isle, the prison home of so many valiant "boys in blue" during the Civil War, the very spot in the lower town where President Lincoln landed on his memorable visit to captured Richmond, when, with loud cries, the race he had enfranchised hailed him as a deliverer; they saw the quaint old Bell House, from which in Colony days had rung the call to debate or to arms; the jail where Aaron Burr was imprisoned for treason—"And served him right," interrupted Jack, who did not admire the brilliant New Yorker since he had heard Hamilton's story—all these they saw, and so many other historic, notable, or modern landmarks that, when all was over, Marian declared her eyes "just ached, seeing things," and Christine dropped into a chair with a sigh of tired content.

But at last, refreshed and rested, they sat after dinner beneath the palms in the Pompeian court of their hotel, and, beside Valentine's marble statue of Jefferson, they listened to the strains of the band-concert in the gallery beyond the great interior court. There they fell to talking over the day's sights and impressions as was their wont; and Roger said:

"It seems strange, does n't it, to see so many monuments to rebels?"

"It should never seem strange, my boy," Uncle Tom replied, "to see monuments to brave and honest men. We are not here as Northerners, but as Americans, and with us it should be as it was with the old Roman who said — what did he say, Bert? *Homo sum* — you know the rest."

And Bert, who, they all declared, welcomed a chance to air his Latin, gave the quotation: "*Homo sum ; humani nihil a me alienum puto.*"

"Which being translated, my beloved hearers," said Jack, "meaneth, 'I 'm with you through thick and through thin.'"

"Oh, Jack! Is n't he just dreadful!" cried Marian. "What does it mean, Bert?"

THE NEW RICHMOND.

A view from the City Hall. Capitol Park, with Crawford's statue of Washington in the foreground.

RICHMOND AT THE CLOSE OF THE CIVIL WAR.

"'I am a man. I think nothing human alien to me,'" translated Bert.

"My, my! hear the boy," cried Jack; "does n't he roll that out finely, though? 'I am a man.' Well, you will be some day, my son."

"Let us hope that you will too, Master Jack," said Uncle Tom. "Now, I would like you all to localize that declaration by Terence, so that it may read: 'I am an American, and to nothing American can I be indifferent.'"

"Well, how does that differ from my free translation?" Jack demanded. "I had the same idea."

"Whatever concerns America should interest us," went on Uncle Tom. "The time has passed for sectionalism. We can all have our opinions as to the right or justice of the Civil War. It simply had to come. It was fought and decided, and all living Americans are now glad of it and rejoice in its conclusions, as they accept its decisions. What was your Decoration Day piece, Jack? You know how it ends — give us the last stanza."

VIEW OF JAMES RIVER FROM
LIBBY HILL.

To which Jack, nothing loath, responded in moderated tones, so as not to disturb those who were listening to the concert :

" For the wreck and the wrong of it, boys and girls,
For the terror and loss, as well,
   Our hearts must hold
   A regret untold
As we think of those who fell.
But their blood, on whichever side they fought,
Re-made the Nation, and Progress brought.
   We forget the woe;
   For we live, and know
That the fighting and sighing,
The falling and dying,
Were but steps toward the Future — the Martyr's
   Way!
Adown which the sons of the Blue and the Gray
   Look, with love and with pride, Decoration Day."

UNION CAVALRYMEN SALUTING THE
MONUMENT OF WASHINGTON.
In Capitol Park.

" That 's about my idea of it," Uncle Tom declared. " So it seems to me, in that spirit Americans should look with interest and appreciation on the memorials of our brave Americans. History hangs by slender threads. Had it not been for Franklin's way of making friends, and thus securing the aid of France in the Revolution, Adams and Henry would have been 'traitors' instead of Arnold, Washington would have been a 'wicked rebel,' and the American Revolution would have been but an insurrection. Americans would have been rearing statues to-day to the De Lanceys and Olivers, whom we now detest as 'tories,' instead of to Prescott and Putnam and Hale and Jefferson — whereas, every one of these was an American, and of certain value to his country — rebel and tory alike. So, too, I can see in the splendid Lee on horseback, on Lee Circle, here in Richmond, the qualities that make for courage, manliness, gallantry, and devotion, quite as much as in the equally striking Grant on horseback in Grant Square in Brooklyn, or the mighty monument that, overtopping all others in the world, in the city that bears his name, testifies to the nation's love and pride in the name and fame of Washington."

The young people were not altogether willing to accept Uncle Tom's theories. Somehow, it seemed to them that to admit virtues in one side took away from the other. But Uncle Tom assured them that such a stand was local, narrow, un-American.

" Be liberal, be broad-minded, boys and girls," he said. " Remember that

8

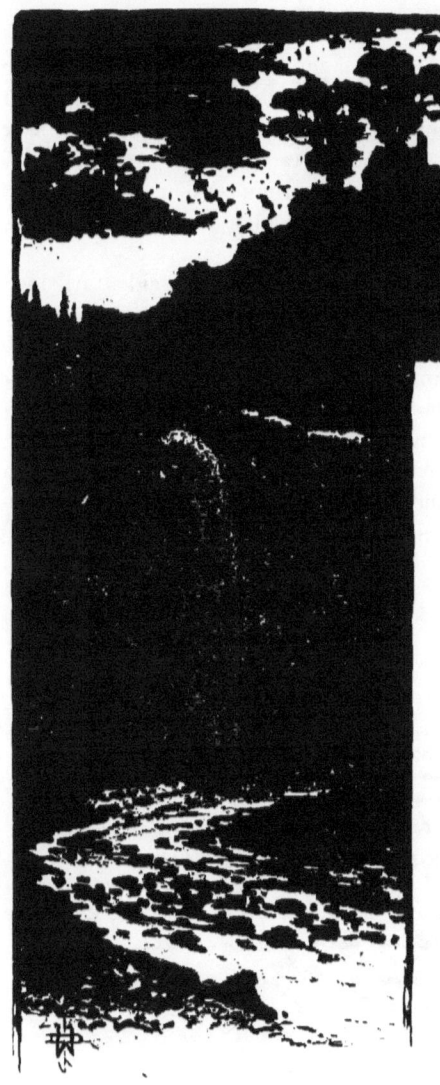

BLOODY RUN, RICHMOND, VA.
Scene of an Indian battle in old Colony days.

loyalty is as much brotherly love as it is hoisting the flag, and that patriotism is as all-embracing as it is assertive. Never tolerate treason; but never forget to forgive. Remember the words of Lincoln, most American of Americans: "We are not enemies, but friends. We must not be enemies. Though passion may have strained, it must not break our bonds of affection. The mystic chords of memory, stretching from every battle-field and patriot grave to every living heart and hearthstone all over this broad land, will yet swell the chorus of the Union, when again touched, as surely they will be, by the better angels of our nature!"

"And yet Lincoln gave the rebels Hail Columbia," declared Jack, reflectively.

"Of course he did," replied Uncle Tom. "It was his duty to preserve the Union, even through blood and tears, and he never faltered. But he never wavered in his great hearted affection for all Americans, either. 'With malice toward none, with charity for all'— that was his plea, even in the hour of victory. Thank God! that 'better nature' which he sought to awaken is now common to all his countrymen, and no true American heart harbors a trace of sectionalism, or limits its love of country to any narrower boundary than that of lake to gulf and ocean to ocean."

Uncle Tom saw that his words had made an impression upon his boys and girls, and he sought by just a final word to broaden and deepen that impression in the way he specially desired.

"So we come back, you see, to where we started," he said. "All men who have shed lustre or brought credit to the American name, or who by gallant deeds, by worthy lives, or by earnest efforts, have helped to make America famous, are famous Americans, whatever their time, their section, or their occupation. Here, in Richmond, while we honor Marshall, the great Chief Justice, and Jefferson, the statesman, we can also honor Lee, the general, or Jackson, the 'Stonewall' hero, or Poe, the poet, who played here as a boy. For all of these men were famous Americans, as well as famous Virginians, and all, in time, will find their rightful places in the righteous verdict of unbiased history."

CLOSING PARAGRAPH OF LINCOLN'S FIRST INAUGURAL ADDRESS.
From original from which the address was delivered.

THOMAS JEFFERSON,

Third President of the United States, and author of the Declaration of Independence

At Charlottesville—Up the Little Mountain—The House with Two Fronts—The Grave on the Mountain—The Story of a Statesman.

ACK stood at the foot of the staircase of the little inn at Charlottesville, and called impatiently up the stairs.

"Come, come, girls! Stop primping!" he cried. "We're bound for a mountain-top, not for the university."

The next moment the door above swung open and the girls came down the stairs, while Marian, in her most dignified manner, said to her brother:

"Jack Dunlap, we scorn your insinuations. We dress just as much to honor dead statesmen as live collegians; so there!"

Roger, ever gallant, sought to rise to the opportunity, and try his luck with a quotation.

"If eyes were made for seeing,
Then beauty is its own excuse for being,"

he remarked, whereupon Jack sank limply into the nearest chair, the girls courtesied profoundly, and Uncle Tom clapped Roger on the back with a laughing "Bravo, Roger! Virginia courtesy must be in the air, and catching."

A ride of four hours the day before had brought the party to picturesque Charlottesville. A restful night in that quiet town had refreshed them greatly, and put them in prime condition to see and enjoy the home of Thomas Jefferson.

The wagonette was at the door, and soon they were speeding out of Charlottesville and along pleasant country roads to the mansion on the mountain-top.

The road wound up the steep hillside, a good three miles from town, though even there the same spirit of progress that they had noted at

"JACK STOOD AT THE FOOT OF THE STAIRCASE."

Richmond seemed to be in evidence, for the town was pushing ambitiously out into what were formerly farms and old estates.

The hill-slopes were green and inviting, the valley was dotted with farms, the little stream across which Thomas Jefferson, as a boy, had often swum his horse, wound through the plain, the woods were brilliant with the contrasting white and red blossoms of the dogwood and the redbud, and everywhere were the delight and beauty of a spring morning in Virginia.

The young folks enjoyed the ride greatly; but Bert said, as the horses breasted the climb, "'Little mountain'! That's what Monticello means, is it? Seems to me it's quite a respectable one. Why, it's almost as steep as a road in the Catskills. I should think Tarleton's troopers must have been pretty well winded if they galloped all the way up this hill just to loot Jefferson's home."

"Oh, did they do that? The mean things!" cried Marian.

"Bert is just a trifle too realistic," said Uncle Tom. "Tarleton and his troopers came tearing up here to capture that pestilent rebel, Jefferson, who was then governor of Virginia. But the governor just managed to give them the slip, and the British colonel kept his hands off the fine old place— it was not so very old then, however,—and did not do much damage."

Jack seemed just a bit dissatisfied. The idea that the British in the Revolution could stay their hands whenever there was a chance to pillage or destroy did not accord with his idea of history.

"I thought that was just the sort of picnic that chump of a Tarleton liked," he said severely.

"Even the worst of us are not so black as we are painted," Uncle Tom declared. "Tarleton has enough sins to his account without adding the looting of Monticello. He held off his hands here, even when Arnold had burned Richmond and Cornwallis had laid waste Jefferson's lowland estate of Edgehill, two or three miles away."

"What were the Americans doing all this time?" asked Jack. "Where were our soldiers?"

"With Washington," Uncle Tom replied. "Virginia was stripped of fighting men at the time of Cornwallis's raid. She was almost bare of resources, too, so lavishly had she contributed to the support of the American army. When the State was invaded by the British,—first by Arnold the traitor and next by Cornwallis and Tarleton,— Jefferson, who was then governor, would not call on Congress or the army for aid, lest Washington's

BACK FROM THE RAID.
"The governor just managed to give them the slip."

forces should be weakened. He himself was no soldier; the militia he summoned were worse than useless; the legislature fled from Richmond to this town of Charlottesville; and along came Cornwallis and Tarleton to bag the whole 'rebel brood.' The militia made themselves scarce; the fugitive legislature followed suit; and Jefferson, making for shelter here at Monticello, had just five minutes' warning, brought by a sort of Virginia Paul Revere, who came tearing up this road to give the alarm. He was just in time, for, as Jefferson galloped down the mountain on one side, he saw the redcoats climbing up the other. He got off, you see, just in the nick of time."

"I should say so!" exclaimed Roger.

"Were his family here?" asked Christine. "How frightened they must have been!"

"They had already hidden their valuables and had been hurried to a safe place," Uncle Tom explained. "Jefferson had then six adopted children in his family — nephews and nieces — and three little motherless girls of his own."

"Well, he did have his hands full," said Jack.

"But he took good care of them and got them all to safe places, while Cornwallis was burning and pillaging his estate of Edgehill," Uncle Tom continued. "After the invasion Jefferson was taken to task for what was claimed to be an indifference to Virginia's security, and even to-day some historians refer contemptuously to his conduct during the British invasion. The truth is, however, that what appeared indifference, and was even called cowardice, was indeed heroism; for Thomas Jefferson knew better than his critics the condition of affairs. It was a case of the few suffering for the many. He felt it to be better even that Virginia should be overrun and laid waste than that the success of the cause for which America was fighting should be jeopardized by a call for help. So he did the best he could with what he had at hand, and his own State came in time to appreciate and acknowledge his wisdom. There are phases of patriotism, boys and girls," Uncle Tom continued, "that are quite different from those with which we are familiar in history. To suffer that good may come, even when that suffering seems needless, or invited, even, may sometimes be, instead, a high order of patriotism."

"DE BRITISH AM COMIN'!"
Hiding the valuables

A DISTANT VIEW OF MONTICELLO.

By this time they had reached the crest of the hill, a spur of Carter Mountain, upon which, perched six hundred feet above the plain, stood the dome-topped mansion of Monticello, the much-loved home of Thomas Jefferson, author of the Declaration of Independence.

The wagonette drew up before the "quarters," and the old negro who has shown the historic house to a generation of visitors met them with garrulous greeting.

"Is this the front?" Marian inquired, going up the broad steps of the western portico.   "Oh, is n't it just lovely!   Where 's the door?"

"No, missey," the old negro replied; "the entrance is cl'ar round on de east front."

"Why, is there another?" asked Marian.   "This looks like the front."

"Well — yes — missey," said the polite old chap, "dis yere 's de r'ar front.   De ra'al front is on de furder side."

They left the "rear front" and walked around to the main entrance of the mansion, the beautiful east front, in which are set the historic clock and weather dial, and which opens into the great hall, once the center of the

THE EAST PORTICO OF MONTICELLO.
"De ra'al front."

master's overflowing hospitality, when Monticello was the Mecca of strangers, admirers, and friends.

The young people, by favor of the present owner, spent a delightful hour in and about the old place examining, inspecting, exclaiming.

They saw the octagonal drawing-room, the great dining-hall, the tea room, and the library; they saw the room occupied by Lafayette, the double-alcoved bed-chamber near to the conservatory, and the room in which Jefferson died. The old negro told them how the house was built, wing by wing, of bricks made on the place, and of timber felled and hewn on the estate. He told them that the plan of the house and the grounds was Jefferson's own, and that even the furniture was designed by him, and much of it made on the place.

"Well, he could do a little of everything, could n't he?" said Roger.

"Indeed he could," Uncle Tom replied. "In head and hand and heart, Thomas Jefferson was a marvel." And then he told the girls what a charming grandfather was the great Democrat. He liked nothing better than a lively romp with his boys and girls, and he was always devising and making all manner of toys and contrivances for them — cupboards and closets, and dishes, and doll-houses, until the little Jeffersons and Randolphs naturally came to the conclusion that "grandpapa" could do about everything.

"I don't blame them," said Christine. "It looks as if he could."

"Of course not many real relics of Jefferson are to be seen about the place to-day," Uncle Tom told them. "Change of owners and the fortunes of war have sadly depleted its belongings and marred its beauty. But it seems to be the desire of the present owner to make the restored mansion as nearly Jeffersonian as possible, and the furnishings of the house are, as you see, on the colonial plan. But, after all, it is the environment that interests. As Monticello is to-day, in situation, outline, atmosphere, and outlook,— in

THE WEST PORTICO OF MONTICELLO.
"The r'ar front."

the real breath of the place,— so it was in the days of its famous master, *plus* the life of a great baronial estate; for that it was in its palmy days, when all the world knew it as the home of the Sage of Monticello."

After they had inspected the house and rambled about the beautiful grounds, Uncle Tom brought them all together at last in the spacious outlook, a stone's throw from the house.

THE HALL AT MONTICELLO.

" My! what a view!" cried Marian.

" Your uncle Thomas had an eye for scenery, had n't he?" said Jack.

" He was a great lover of natural scenery," Uncle Tom replied.   " Even in France, where he did and saw so much, he was always pining for what he called his Virginia wilderness on the mountain-top."

They sat silent for a while enjoying the scene.   Hillside and valley, as the boys and girls looked out upon them, were green with all the verdant beauty of a Virginia spring.   Great trees rose above them on the far-spreading lawns.   Redbud and lilacs, dogwood and golden willow, gave color and fragrance, while redbreasts hopped about on the grass or swung and whistled on the branches above them.

Below them stretched the valley, where to the right Uncle Tom located for them Shadwell, the birthplace of Jefferson, Edgehill, his other estate, and, farther off, Montpellier, the home of yet another President of the United States — his successor, James Madison.   To the west, the long spur of the Blue Ridge rose from the basin-like valley, while above this ridge could be traced the faint, far-distant line of the Alleghanies.   Almost at their feet lay Charlottesville, and, just beyond the town, they could see, peeping from its screen of trees, the clustered buildings of the University of Virginia, founded by Jefferson in his later days, and almost as dear to his heart as the Declaration of Independence itself.

"What a lovely, lovely spot!" said Christine, upon whom the place and its associations made a deep impression. "I'd rather live here than at the White House."

"Jefferson was much of your opinion, my dear," Uncle Tom declared. "The White House of his day was little more than a great, draughty, white barn; and, yet, it was the White House rather than this charming Monticello that linked Jefferson's name to fame."

"Ting-a-ling, ting-a-ling-ling!" cried Jack, swinging an imaginary bell. "All aboard for a biography cruise! Heave ahead, Uncle Tom! Here's just the spot to give us Jefferson's story."

"It must be condensed into brief space, then," said Uncle Tom; "for we shall need to start on our return ride speedily."

So Uncle Tom sketched rapidly for them the outline of Thomas Jefferson's career. He told them of the young Virginian's boyhood and youth, into which, though earnest and painstaking, the boy managed to get a good deal of fun and out-of-door life, and learned to love the woods, the fields, and the farm; he told them how Jefferson gained success as a young lawyer, and at last ventured into public life; how, at twenty-six, he became a member of the Virginia House of Burgesses; and how, when he went into politics, he was both prudent and honest, and made a vow never to be drawn into speculation

THE MAIN STAIRWAY AT MONTICELLO.

or "jobs," or be anything but just "a farmer"; and, through fifty years of public life, Uncle Tom assured them, Jefferson kept his vow.

"Then, politicians did speculate and make money out of their opportunities in Jefferson's time, eh?" queried Jack. "Why, I thought these were the degenerate days, and that every one was angelic in the good old times."

"My dear Jack," said Uncle Tom, "there is not a phase of public dishonesty or political intrigue to-day but had its parallel in what are wrongly called the good old days. You know my theory; we are an improvement on our ancestors in every way — morally, physically, and intellectually."

"Hear, hear, hear!" cried Jack.

"Oh, Uncle Tom!" exclaimed Christine. "Is that so? Better than Washington?"

"Don't hold me to individual cases, my dear," said Uncle Tom. "I speak collectively. The world progresses in everything that works for good. In spite of all the unpleasantnesses we daily see, in spite of all the hard things we hear, we are better than the folks of those so-called 'good old days.' In the story of the past it is the good only that survives. We do not see or else we do not heed the evil. Distance always lends enchantment alike to past and future — the was and the is-to-be. But here! let me get on with Jefferson. He was not very well off as a young man, but in 1772 he married a rich wife, and his two thousand acres increased to forty thousand. Then it was that he built Monticello, turned his 'little mountain' into a park, and became a landed proprietor."

"I thought he was called the Great Democrat," said Bert.

"He was," replied Uncle Tom; "but more from the principles he laid down and the measures for which he worked than from any simplicity in living or surroundings. His love of personal liberty grew with the years. He heard Patrick Henry give his great Richmond speech, and became a fiery patriot. When Washington was made commander-in-chief, Jefferson was sent to Congress in his place, and there prepared and presented the famous document with which his name is chiefly connected — the Declaration of Independence."

"I have seen the desk on which he wrote the De-

JEFFERSON'S CHAIR AND WRITING-TABLE.

claration of Independence," Roger announced with due impressiveness. "It belongs to one of his descendants in Boston."

"And when we were in Philadelphia, Roger," declared Jack, solemnly, "I saw as many as four million descendants of the fellows who put the Declaration through Congress."

"What do you mean, Jack?" said Roger. "Philadelphia people? Where did you get four million?"

"No; Philadelphia flies, my son," was Jack's reply.

"Oh, Jack Dunlap!" exclaimed Marian. "Don't be ridiculous."

"No; honor bright, it 's so," Jack asserted. "A man there told me that this very Thomas Jefferson declared that the final vote on the Declaration of Independence was hastened by the flies that came in swarms from a near-by stable and nearly pestered the lives of the Congressmen those hot July days. So the delegates just hurried things, to get out of the way of the flies."

JEFFERSON'S DOUBLE-ALCOVE BEDROOM.

"Is that really so, Uncle Tom?" asked Marian, a bit doubtfully.

"Well, Jack tells it, and Jack is an investigator, you know." Uncle Tom replied diplomatically.

"Then, I should think," said Bert, "that, instead of the eagle, the fly should be the national 'bird' of America. He made us free, if he put the Declaration through."

DESK ON WHICH THE DECLARATION OF INDEPENDENCE WAS WRITTEN.
From a drawing by Thomas Jefferson.

"What an absurd lot of boys you are!" said Marian. "Do drop fairy tales and let Uncle Tom go on with facts."

"Well, I like that!" said Jack. "I tell you my fly story was fact, Marian Dunlap. We get it straight from the Sage of Monticello himself."

"The Sage of Monticello!" cried Marian scornfully. "As if Jefferson would say such a ridiculous thing as that."

"That 's the trouble with girls," remarked Jack. "They always will doubt the truth of history."

"But that fly story is n't history, is it, Uncle Tom?" said Marian.

"Well — Jefferson, like Franklin, had an excellent sense of humor," said Uncle Tom. "So it may be that he is responsible for Jack's fly story, just as he is responsible for lifting out of a Latin comic poem our splendid national motto of *E Pluribus Unum.*"

"Oh, yes ; I remember how we came across that story in Washington," said Christine.

"For further particulars inquire of Mr. Albertus Uphamus, our lexicon fiend," said Jack. "Push ahead with grandpapa Jefferson, Uncle Tom."

"Well," said his uncle, again picking up his biographical thread, "Jefferson declined a reëlection to Congress, believing he could best serve the cause by keeping his State progressing toward liberty and self-government. So he went into the Virginia legislature, and for nearly two years worked away on a constitution for the new State. He was always proud of this work, especially of the clause that established religious freedom in Virginia. That may seem to you, now, a simple affair, not even open to argument ; but it took a long, hard fight to get it through. Things were different in Jefferson's day. Bigotry and sectarianism have almost died out in our hundred and twenty years of freedom. Another sign of progress, you see, boys and girls. America has no place in this enlightened day for the bias of bigotry or the enigma of exclusion. It was these that Jefferson ever fought against, and against them all real Americans should earnestly protest, as we stand at the dawn of a new and yet more glorious century of power and progress."

Uncle Tom spoke earnestly, and the young people, though they did not catch his full meaning, applauded his sentiment and honored him with an emphatic "That 's so !"

"In 1779," said Uncle Tom, "Jefferson was elected governor, and soon after had to stand the strain of British invasion of which I told you, which so nearly culminated in his capture. After his term closed he refused reëlection, thinking that a soldier was a better head for the State just then. His wife died, and he came here to Monticello sad and heartbroken ; but he was not permitted to remain here long. His country demanded his services. He was sent to Congress, where he invented the dollars and dimes of our national currency, which, before, had been pounds, shillings, and pence."

"Good for him !" cried Jack, "He was right up-to-date and American, was n't he ? "

"None more so in his day," Uncle Tom replied. "In 1784 he was sent as American Minister to France and returned in 1789 to go into President Washington's cabinet as Secretary of State. He resigned in 1794, because he and Hamilton could not agree, and thus helped to invent politics in Amer-

9

ica, for out of this disagreement came the two political parties of his day. In 1796 he was elected Vice-President, and in 1800 he was elected President of the United States."

"Well, he kept going right up, did n't he?" said Roger.

"That 's the time he rode horseback to the capitol, hitched his horse to the picket fence, and just went in to be inaugurated, is n't it?" queried Jack.

LAFAYETTE.
The statue by Bartholdi in Union Square, New York.

"All of which reads very nicely, but I 'm afraid it is n't altogether fact," said Uncle Tom. "He meant to ride to his inauguration in his own fine coach and four, but his turnout did not get to Washington from Monticello in time. So he went—some say on horseback, others say, in a hired coach just like any other President, and was inaugurated with just as much display and noise and jubilee."

"Well, how did that horseback story get into history then?" inquired Jack.

"From a later occurrence, I imagine," Uncle Tom replied. "When Madison, his successor, was inaugurated, Jefferson and his sixteen-year old grandson rode on horseback to the capitol, hitched their horses to the palings, and went in to see the show. The two occasions have simply got mixed, you see."

"That 's so. Now, what were the biggest things he did as President?" asked Roger.

"The biggest things, as you would call them," said Uncle Tom, "were, I suppose, when he sent Decatur and his sailors to say to the Dey of Algiers, 'No, sir! we won't pay tribute'; the purchase of Louisiana from Napoleon Bonaparte, who was then rising to great power in France; and the embargo of 1807, which Jefferson always held, if strictly kept, would have prevented the war of 1812."

"Would it?" asked Bert.

"That 's an open question," Uncle Tom replied. "If all men had been Jeffersons it might have served his purposes; but men are not alike, and de-

MONTICELLO HOSPITALITY.

signs frequently go wrong — as in this case. After his two terms as President, Jefferson came home here to Monticello — but not to be left alone. He was kept busy being hospitable, and it well nigh ruined him. His affairs became so involved that, in his last years, he was in desperate straits for money; he nearly lost Monticello, and had to sell his great library to supply his needs. He died on the Fourth of July, 1826 — the fiftieth anniversary of the Declaration of Independence, which owed its form and language to him."

IN THE BALL-ROOM AT MONTICELLO.

"That was odd, was n't it?" said Roger.

"It was certainly a coincidence," replied Uncle Tom; "but it was emphasized still more by the fact that on the same day his fellow-worker, old-time friend, political rival, and brother-patriot, John Adams, died in his Massachusetts home — his last words a thought of Jefferson."

"Give us Daniel Webster, Jack," said Bert, as they all rose from their seats in the outlook. So, and as they walked down the road to the monument, Jack, obligingly, as ever, recited for them there, under the Virginia sky, upon that forest-clothed hill-slope of Monticello, the great orator's tribute to these two "fathers of the republic":

"'Their fame is safe. That is now treasured up beyond the reach of accident. Although no sculptured marble should rise to their memory, nor engraved stone bear record of their deeds, yet will their remembrance be as lasting as the land they honored. Marble columns may indeed moulder into dust, time may erase all impress from the crumbling stone, but their fame remains; for with American liberty it rose, and with American liberty only can it perish.'"

And Uncle Tom responded with a solemn "Amen!"

They halted before the iron-fenced enclosure by the roadway down the mountain and looked upon the simple ten-foot obelisk that rises above the dust of the third President of the United States.

"Not much of a marble column about this," was Jack's comment.

Bert read aloud the inscription on the pedestal:

"'Here lies buried Thomas Jefferson, author of the Declaration of American Independence, of the statutes of Virginia for Religious Freedom, and Father of the University of Virginia.'"

"Is n't that splendid!" said Christine, impressed alike by the simplicity and meaning of the inscription.

"Those three things, I suppose," Marian remarked, "are what folks consider the greatest things he did."

THE GRAVE OF THOMAS JEFFERSON.

"So considered by himself," Uncle Tom explained. "In fact, that inscription was composed by Jefferson himself, and found among his papers after his death."

As the wagonette took them up, and they drove down this historic hillside toward Charlottesville, Uncle Tom, in a few words, summed up the famous man whose home they had seen: "A great leader, a great American, a great man," he said. "With an unwavering faith in the will of the people as the sole law of the land, he became, for our republic, the typical democrat, —a believer in the theory of government by the people. Politically a mighty factor in American history, he was personally a delightful man, benevolent and intelligent, cheery of manner and placid in disposition; he was never angry, fretful, or discontented; he was happiest when helping others,

IN CHARLOTTESVILLE.

and one of his chief rules of conduct was ' never to trouble another
for what he could do himself.' "

At this Marian bent forward
and nudged, significantly, her brother.

" Very good advice, my dear,"
said Jack, the incorrigible. " Please
see that you follow it."

That afternoon, they took the
trolley quite to the other end of
this picturesque old town of Charlottesville, to visit the delightfully
situated University of Virginia —
the child of Jefferson's later years,
founded by him, endowed by his
exertions, and ever loyal to his
memory.

Uncle Tom and his "pilgrims"
wandered about the beautiful
grounds, unrivalled in situation and
unsurpassed in view. They walked
the cool and shady colonnades before the students' low-roofed dormitories;
they studied the curious curved brick walls enclosing certain sections of the

grounds — a Jeffersonian contrivance to economize bricks, and yet have strength and durability; they visited the museum and saw the remnants of the library and the marble statue of the founder, saved by the students from the fire that destroyed

IN THE UNIVERSITY GROUNDS

These walls are one brick thick, the winding form is taken for supposed economy of material

the famous Rotunda, designed by Jefferson. The Rotunda and annex still lay in ruins, but a nobler structure they were told was soon to rise thereon, and other buildings of modern design and finish. They "did their manners" for a while in the cool drawing-room of one of the courteous Professors; they strolled about East Lawn and West Lawn—the double "Campus" of the college, as Bert called it; they visited the gymnasium and the athletic field, in which the boys were especially interested. Indeed, when he had talked with some of "the fellows," and compared notes of records and achievements, Jack declared that he did n't wonder that, in the excitement of the fire, twelve of those "plucky chaps" had in a few minutes taken down and carried out, without a break, the heavy marble statue of Jefferson, which it had taken the contractors many hours and much ingenuity to erect.

THE UNIVERSITY OF VIRGINIA AT CHARLOTTESVILLE.

The central rotunda, designed by Jefferson, was destroyed by fire in 1895

"I tell you," he said, "excitement does a good deal, but sand does more, and these university fellows have a lot of it. They 're just A 1 ball players, and I don't wonder. Look at what they 've got here in grounds and scenery. I tell you they can build men down here in Virginia. Three cheers for the mother of Presidents! Run up the flag for Thomas Jefferson!"

IN THE COLONNADE OF THE UNIVERSITY.

KENTUCKY HOSPITALITY IN THE OLDEN TIME

Over the Hills into Kentucky — The Three Giants — The Champion of a Mistake — Calhoun's Story — The "Millboy of the Slashes" — Blue-grass Landscapes — Ashland, the Home of Henry Clay.

THE boys and girls long remembered their westward way from Charlottesville.

Up hill and down dale, climbing heavy grades, piercing mountain passes, while the afternoon grew into sunset and the sunset into glorious moonlight, the train sped on, now giving broad vistas of the Piedmont lowlands, stretched like a panorama beneath them, now showing peak after peak of the forest-clad Blue Ridge, piled far above them, until they crossed the wide Shenandoah Valley, and climbed the farther slopes of the Alleghanies. A constant succession of "Oh!" and "Ah!" of "Look!" and "See!" kept eye and tongue busy, as picturesque views of mountain and valley, farm land, village, and hillside clearing followed fast upon each other; and when at last the dark settled down, and in the highlands, where peak seemed crowded against peak, the mountain-tops were ringed with fire, the children accepted this disastrous illumination as a spectacle specially prepared for their benefit, and thanked Uncle Tom for so dramatic a finale.

As for Uncle Tom, he was watchful for whatever, on this delightful car ride, might interest his young charges. He pointed out to them as they drew away from Charlottesville the last glimpse of Monticello perched on its distant hill-top; he showed them in what direction, miles to the south, lay Appomattox, and, farther still, Red Hill, the pleasant plantation home of Patrick Henry, champion of Independence. As they crossed the valley of the Shenandoah each one of the five wished to break out with "Sheridan's Ride," but could not for the views that claimed their attention; and as they drew up at Staunton Station, Uncle Tom told them that forty miles to the

A VIRGINIA BY-WAY.
In the Virginia lowlands.

south rose that surprising rock freak, the " Natural Bridge,' up which young
George Washington once climbed to cut his name, high above that of all
other visitors.

So they journeyed on into the health-giving regions of the Virginia
springs ; and as they sat at supper in the comfortable dining-car, Uncle Tom
fell to talking of the new region they were to enter during the night, while
they, as Jack expressed it, " lay sleeping at the rate of forty miles an hour,"
as, after crossing the Alleghanies, they would descend into the fertile region
of Kentucky, the heroic land of American history.

" The dark and bloody ground, — was n't it called that ? " asked Roger.

" The home of Daniel Boone," cried Jack.

" And of Henry Clay," said Bert.

" Henry Clay ? " queried Christine ; " is n't he the man who said, ' I had
rather be right than President ? ' "

" Tell us about him, Uncle Tom," said Marian.   " Can we see where
he lived ? "

" That 's the next thing on the docket," Uncle Tom replied.   " I hope
to show you Ashland to-morrow."

" But see here," he said, as, a few minutes later, they sat in the unoccu-
pied saloon compartment of their car, which they now and then, as Bert
explained, "preëmpted for a conference," "what can you boys and girls
tell me about Henry Clay ? Who was he ? "

They really could n't tell so very much when thus brought to book.
Bert said that Clay was called the great Kentuckian, though just why, he

HENRY CLAY AT THE AGE OF FORTY-THREE.

When he was Speaker of the House of Representatives.

NEAR CALHOUN'S HOME.

did n't know, unless he was Kentucky's greatest man. Roger thought he was Webster's rival in the Senate, though precisely over what Roger could n't tell unless it was in the desire to be President. Jack said he was called the "mill-boy of the Slashes," though just what that meant Jack really could n't say.

As for the girls, Marian was positive that Clay had something to do with the Missouri Compromise, which kept the nation from fighting over slavery, and Christine knew he was Secretary of State and two or three times was defeated for the Presidency, although he was the most popular man in the country, which, so Christine declared, seemed to her very odd indeed.

Uncle Tom smiled approval at these attempts to locate Henry Clay, as he called them, although he felt forced to confess that the information was a trifle vague as to foundations and reasons.

"But, then," he added, "your misty conception of one of the most popular leaders in American politics is but a reflection of the cloudiness that veils all the men of what might be termed the middle ages of American history. The fathers of the republic still stand out clear and strong; but the giants of the "forties"— Clay, Webster, Calhoun — are little more than a memory, scarce more, indeed, than names to the mass of Americans to-day. But, you see, failure begets forgetfulness, and these three men, because they failed of their chief ambition,— the Presidency,— fail of due recognition. It does not seem right, but perhaps it is just. I doubt now if you can tell me as much about Calhoun as you did of Clay. Can you?"

There was silence a moment. Then Bert said:

"Was n't he called 'the great Nullifier'? Did n't he believe so thoroughly in State Sovereignty and State Rights that he came very near breaking up the Union?"

Uncle Tom nodded.

"Was n't he Vice-President?" asked Christine.

"Yes; for two terms," Uncle Tom replied.

"And a Southerner with a great head of hair?" asked Marian.

"Right," was the answer; "at least, his best-known pictures pile up the hair, though the best-known, you remember, are not always the best in fact."

"Well, I guess that 's all we know of the gentleman," said Jack. "Bert can go up head."

"It is n't very much to know, though; do you think so?" was Uncle Tom's comment. "And yet, in his day," he added, "John C. Calhoun was

JOHN C. CALHOUN.

as great a force in American history as Daniel Webster, as notable a personality as Henry Clay. Honored, almost idolized by his State, followed by a host of supporters, his career was, nevertheless, a great mistake, and posterity, as I have assured you, never perpetuates mistakes. It is only success that succeeds."

"Now, Uncle Tom," cried Christine, "you know you don't believe that.

CALHOUN'S OFFICE AND HOME AT FORT HILL, SOUTH CAROLINA.
Now on the grounds of Clemson Agricultural College.

How many times have you repeated for us that poem of Story's — 'Io Victis,' is n't it?"

"Oh, yes; a fine thing!" exclaimed Jack. "I know it, too:

'I sing the hymn of the conquered, who fell in the battle of life —'"

"All right, Jack," said Uncle Tom, restraining his nephew's oratory: "I don't know, however, that that exactly fits Calhoun's case. You see, he succeeded to a certain extent, and out of his apparent success came America's greatest stress and bloodiest struggle for existence. And yet, Calhoun's life story is that of an earnest and honest endeavor toward what he deemed just, right, and patriotic ends. Action depends largely upon the point of view, and to his standpoint the world has given the verdict of 'a mistake.' But John C. Calhoun was a famous American; he is South Carolina's most eminent son, and is well worth our study and remembrance."

"He was a disunion man, was n't he?" objected Bert.

"He was an earnest and outspoken States' Rights man," Uncle Tom replied. "He held that each State was an independent power, and had the right, under the Constitution, to act for itself, even to act contrary to — or what is called 'nullify'— a law of the nation."

"From *ne ullus*, not any," interpolated the philological Bert. "That means, not amounting to anything, useless, not binding."

"In other words, N. G.," said Jack; "make it brief, professor."

"To us Calhoun's doctrine sounds revolutionary," Uncle Tom continued. "It was; but all such beliefs, as we look back upon them, were really necessary to the proper development of the real strength of the republic. Obstacles help us to remove obstacles, you know, and the path of abiding union lay through attempted disunion."

"That sounds odd," said Roger.

"It would if it were n't Uncle Tom who says it," Christine declared. "He always sees a good side to everything."

"We must, my dear," said Uncle Tom, smiling. "Why else should things occur? I remember somewhere having seen a verse that fits here:

"To that clearer sight
The rim of shadow
Is the line of light.

Do you know what that means? Well, you will, later. And let me say for Calhoun and his followers that they acted from what they deemed right motives. Even though he was the chief and most eloquent advocate of slavery, he was so from principle, and while abhorring his conclusions, we should honor his integrity. No man ever questioned Calhoun's sincerity, and he certainly had what is called the courage of his convictions."

CALHOUN'S OFFICE ON HIS FORT HILL ESTATE.

"But that is what we wish to forget him for," said Marian. "Is n't there something we can remember him for?"

"Certainly," replied Uncle Tom. "Calhoun first proposed the annexation of Texas, and he kept the nation from a third war with England, in 1848, over the vexed question of the Oregon boundary. These are both what the boys would call 'feathers in his cap,' and are well worth remembering."

"Where did he live?" Christine inquired.

"In the very uppermost corner of South Carolina, just where the State lies like a wedge between North Carolina and Georgia. Calhoun, you know, was South Carolina born and bred. He was Secretary of War under President Monroe, and Secretary of State under Tyler. He was Vice-President for two terms, with John Quincy Adams and Andrew Jackson. While he was Secretary of War he removed to this estate in the wedge of South Carolina. It was called Fort Hill, and was a quaint old Southern mansion, very much like Mount Vernon.

A HERO OF THE FORTIES.

General Samuel Houston, first President of Texas.

"The estate now belongs to an agricultural college and the old mansion is, I believe, used as the college museum and post office. Not far from the house still stands the little office or library in which the great Nullifier did his thinking, reading, and working."

"The same as on the Webster place," Christine reminded them.

"There were numerous things that were almost coincidences in the careers of those three great Senators, Clay, Webster, and Calhoun," Uncle Tom replied. "Each was a leader, each aspired to the highest place in the nation, each failed of success. They were all born at the same period — about 1780; all three died at the same period — about 1850. A comparative study of their lives is of great interest, for their influence upon their times was great."

"Tell us about Henry Clay, Uncle Tom," said Bert. "You began to, you know, and then switched off on Calhoun."

"You 're a great fellow to stick to the main subject, Bert," said Uncle Tom, with a laugh. "That 's all right; I like to see it in you. It means a clear mind and persistence — two qualities to keep a man active and bring him to success."

"Oh, that 's Bert, every time, Uncle Tom," cried Jack. "He 's a master mind. He 'll be President yet. Don't go back on your friends, will you, old fellow?"

"Nor on your convictions, either, Bert," said Uncle Tom. "That is what has wrecked too many reputations and brought too many public men to

ASHLAND, THE HOME OF HENRY CLAY.

grief. Now as to Henry Clay. His story is one of popularity and progress, tinctured with failure. He was a poor boy, born in the Virginia lowlands, at a place called the Slashes, in Hanover county, a short distance north of Richmond. He was the fifth in a family of seven, and one of his 'chores' was to ride the horse to mill; hence, the "mill-boy of the Slashes," you see. He was a bright, wide-awake boy, and finally managed to get to Richmond and start out in life as a lawyer. In 1797 he decided to try his fortunes in

10

a new region, and removed across the mountains into Kentucky, settling in Lexington — the town for which we are bound."

"I 'll bet he did n't go in a parlor car, though," said Jack.

"Of course he did n't," said Marian. "Why, they did n't even have steam-cars then, did they, Uncle Tom?"

"No, no; it was 1830, at least, before the railway pierced these hills," Uncle Tom replied, "nearly forty years after Clay crossed the mountains. You may be sure that Henry Clay went on horseback, as did most people then, along the old highway to the West that had been made out of the trail of trappers and pioneers. He soon became popular in Kentucky. He had a frank, cordial way about him that made friends quickly, and before long he was in politics. He was sent to the legislature in 1804, where he advocated the gradual abolition of slavery. In 1806 he was sent to the Senate of the United States."

the Diny of Ashland.

"A senator so soon!" cried Bert. "Why, how old was he?"

"Not quite thirty," was Uncle Tom's reply. "But young men of promise quickly got to the front in those days."

"I should say so," said Roger.

"Why were n't we living then?" remarked Jack.

"From that time on, for more than forty years, Henry Clay was a public man, either in the Senate, the House of Representatives, or the Cabinet. He was three times Speaker of the House of Representatives; he was Secretary of State under President John Quincy Adams; he was one of the commissioners to sign the Treaty of Ghent that closed the War of 1812. From first to last his policy was popular, because it was what is called American."

"Meaning by that?" queried Bert.

"Meaning by that," replied Uncle Tom: "'the best for America, and America the best!' I don't mean that he went about bragging and 'spoiling for a fight,' as the saying is; he was n't, by any means, one of those chip-on-the-shoulder people sometimes called 'Jingoes'; I mean that he labored for the welfare of the republic in whose future he so ardently believed. Henry Clay made mistakes, and had many shortcomings, but from first to last he was an American: national, broad-minded, patriotic, proud of his country, ardently devoted to the Union, earnest and eloquent for every measure or policy likely to advance American nationality—from curbing the tyranny of England in 1812 to struggling to keep the Union unbroken in 1850."

"That 's the kind of man I like," cried Jack. "Why under the sun was n't he President?"

"Simply because he was n't elected, Jack," said Uncle Tom.

"Well, it was a shame," Jack declared. "He was better than half the fellows who were elected."

"A man who is so ardent and so splendid a party chief as was Henry Clay," said Uncle Tom, "also makes many enemies. The crowds cheered for 'the mill-boy of the Slashes' and 'Harry of the West,' as they loved to call their magnetic leader, but he always just failed of nomination or election. For twenty years the prize of the Presidency dangled before the eyes of Henry Clay only to be snatched away by less able men, and always to accomplish the very desire which Clay had most at heart—harmony and union. When you read American political history, you will understand why so popular a leader never became anything but a fallen idol."

"I don't see it," exclaimed Jack, hotly. Jack seemed already to have become a Clay partizan by inspiration, Uncle Tom declared. "He did n't fall. The people who went back on him fell," said Jack.

THE PARK AT ASHLAND.

"Good for you, Jack!" cried Uncle Tom, who always did admire enthusiasm. "I like to see earnestness, even when I am not thoroughly in accord with it. Your remark, too, though your own, singularly enough is
exactly what Henry Clay's admirers said. I wonder if I can recall a spirited
bit of verse by an ardent Clay man — William Wilberforce Lord. I got
by heart once because then I believed it. Mr. Stedman considers it as
as Whittier's lines on Webster. Let's see how it sounds to-day. It w
written after Clay's overthrow, and was called 'On the Defeat of a Gre..
Man.'"

And Uncle Tom, leaning back against the comfortable cushions of the
compartment, recalled Lord's spirited lines:

> "Fallen! How fallen? States and empires fall;
>   O'er towers and rock-built walls,
> And perished nations, floods and tempests call
> With hollow sound along the sea of time:
>   The great man never falls;—
> He lives, he towers aloft, he stands sublime:
>   *They fall*, who give him not
> The honor here that suits his future name,—
>   They die and are forgot.

"O giant, loud and blind! the great man's fame
Is his own shadow and not cast by thee;
A shadow that shall grow
As down the heaven of time the sun descends,
And on the world shall throw
His godlike image till it sinks, where blends
Time's dim horizon with Eternity."

"Fine, but not Whittier," was the verdict of Roger of Boston.

"It's true, all the same," said Jack. "Great heads, eh— yours truly and Mr. Lord?"

"Come back here a hundred years from now, Jack," Uncle Tom suggested, "and see how your hero's fame stands the test of time. That, after all, is the real standard of greatness."

With that they separated for the night, and next morning were up bright and early for their first glimpse of Kentucky, as they sped on from the eastern foot-hills toward Lexington, in the heart of the blue-grass country.

"Why is it called blue-grass, Uncle Tom?" asked Marian. "It looks greener than green to me — and how beautiful and velvety."

"Later in the year you get the blue effect that gives this famous Kentucky grass its name," Uncle Tom replied. "When the wind bends the high grass, you catch the tint that underlies the green and gives a bluish tinge to the waving blades."

"But that man in the smoking-compartment just told me," said Bert, "that the blue grass was not of Kentucky origin. He says it was brought here from Indiana, but that the Kentucky soil has seemed particularly adapted to its development. Is that so, Uncle Tom?"

"Give it up," his uncle replied. "I am not up in botanical history, as our friend in the smoking-room seems to be. Perhaps he is right; but for ll purposes, sentimental, picturesque, and practical, the blue grass is especially a Kentucky product, and will always be associated with this fertile region."

HENRY CLAY'S INKSTAND.

They reached Lexington and their hotel in time for breakfast, and, soon after, sauntered up and down broad, prosperous-looking Main Street for a glance at the attractive town.

Roger seemed inclined to resent its size and importance.

"Why, it's bigger than our Lexington," he said, with the tone of one who thought that *the* Lexington of America should be the historical town surrounding the storied Middlesex green.

"To be sure it is," said Uncle Tom.   "This Lexington leads your Lexington by nearly twenty thousand people.   It is a business center, you can see, Roger, and a thriving, go-ahead city.   But let this satisfy you — it was named for your Lexington in Massachusetts.   For while the settlers were laying out their town, the tidings came to them of that famous fight that opened the American Revolution, and at once they gave to the new Kentucky settlement the name of that far-off Massachusetts battle-field."

"Good for them!" cried Jack.   "There's appreciation for you, Roger."

"That was fine, was n't it?" said Roger, highly satisfied with the information; and as they boarded a trolley in front of the Breckenridge statue on their way to Ashland, the Boston boy raised his cap in salute to the enterprising Kentucky city, which he called "Sam Adams's stepson."

A ride of a mile along broad and pleasant Main Street brought them to a turn in the road from where it was only a short walk to the estate famous throughout America under its name of "Ashland."

The "old Kentucky home" of Henry Clay lay at a very slight elevation in the midst of broad and far-reaching pastures, while all about the house itself clustered a stately growth of ash, oak, and walnut trees.

The house stood back some distance from the road, a broad driveway leading to the ample front door.

But here again, as in the Webster case, the children learned that they were not looking upon the real Clay house.   That, so Uncle Tom informed them, was torn down years ago because no longer safe, the small, yellow building off in the fields being the only real survivor of Henry Clay's day.

"Well, here's a curious thing!" said Jack, standing still beneath a great ash, and pushing back his cap in surprise.   "Do you notice the coincidence, Uncle Tom? Clay, Webster, and Calhoun—three statesmen of the same age and time — each one of them in the Senate — each in the Cabinet — each hoping to be President — each one a farmer on a big estate — the house of each one practically wiped out of existence after the death of the owner, and, standing not far from the house, the only real relic in each case—a solitary little yellow building, used by its former owner as his study or office. Now, is n't that odd?"

The whole party exclaimed at the curious coincidence, and Uncle Tom remarked:

"It is as I told you, Jack, when we were talking over Calhoun's story. The similarity in the lives of these three great statesmen, though they were so absolutely different as personalities, is marked and striking.   But,

CLAY'S WALK AT ASHLAND.

I confess, I had not seen or known of all these points that you bring out."
You have a sharp eye for 'curios', old fellow."

The door of the mansion was flung open in hospitable welcome, and
under the guidance of an affable colored butler the children were shown
through the handsome house, every room of which is eloquent with memorials of the great man who once called Ashland " home."

The house, they were glad to know, was in almost every respect an exact
and faithful reproduction of the original Clay mansion, built by "the great
pacificator" in 1809.

But, even more than the house, the surroundings of the house spoke of
the famous Kentuckian.   Here, at least, were things that actually environed

HENRY CLAY IN 1844.
When he was nominated for the Presidency of the United States

him, and in which he delighted — the tall pines transplanted by him from the Kentucky mountains; the winding path that was his favorite walk, tree-shaded and shrub-bordered, just as arranged by him; the wide stretches of pasture land beyond the house, which, as in the founder's day, give the finest grazing-ground in the world to a blooded stock that has become famous in horse-history.

A MIRROR FROM ASHLAND.
Now in possession of John M. Clay, Esq.

Boys and girls alike were "simply crazy," as their extravagant language declared, over the beautiful Kentucky horses, which had been an increasing feature in the landscape ever since their descent from the east Kentucky highlands. But the Lexington horses, so Jack affirmed, "just walk away with them all."

Beyond the town, through a frame of leafy walnut branches, Uncle Tom, as he stood with his young people on the violet-studded Ashland lawn, pointed out to them, two miles away, the tall column of the Clay monument in the Lexington cemetery.

Leaving beautiful Ashland, the tourists boarded a trolley back to town, and, a mile to the north, as Ashland was a mile to the south, they came to the grave of a true American.

The towering marble shaft, topped by the ever-familiar figure of Henry Clay, the lawmaker, sprang into the air from a pedestal that was the tomb. Within this rectangular room the children saw, through the gate of open iron-work, the marble sarcophagi that held the remains of Henry Clay and his devoted wife. Encircled by a wreath carved upon one draped sarcophagus stood the simple announcement: HENRY CLAY; while on the base of the supporting pedestal these words were read — a message from the dead statesman to his fellow-Americans:

"I can with unshaken confidence appeal to the divine Arbiter for the truth of the declaration that I have been influenced by no impure purpose, no personal motive, have sought no personal aggrandizement, but that in all my public acts I have had a sole and single eye and a warm, devoted heart directed and dedicated to what, in my best judgment, I believe to be the true interests of my country."

"Well, I guess that's so, is n't it?" was Bert's comment, as, at last, they turned from the grave of Clay and walked down the grassy slope.

A BLUE-GRASS MEADOW PASTURE.

" Yes; I believe it is," his uncle replied.   " With all his inconsistencies,
Henry Clay was immovable in one thing: his devotion to the Union.   Almost his last public words were a plea for harmony.   ' Let us,' he said, ' discard
all resentments, all passions, all petty jealousies, all personal desires, all love of
place, all hungering after the gilded crumbs which fall from the table of
power . . . . and think alone of our God, our country, our conscience, and our
glorious Union.' "

" That was fine," said Roger ; " but they did n't mind him."

" No ; they did n't," Uncle Tom replied.   " The conflict between freedom
and slavery was inevitable.   It had to come, and not even the loving appeal
of the great peacemaker could stop, although it did for a time stay, it.   If it
had come in his day I am certain he would have been found on the side of
Union.   There only could he stand who gave voice to this as the sentiment
of his old age: ' So long as it pleases God to give me a voice to express
my sentiments, or an arm, weak and enfeebled as it may be by age, that
voice and that arm will be on the side of my country, for the support of the
general authority and for the maintenance of the powers of this Union.' "

" Henry Clay," continued Uncle Tom, as once again they took the trolley
and, watching the tall Clay shaft recede in a verdant perspective, buzzed

back to town, "was a notable figure in the history of the republic. Imperious, headstrong, brilliant, imaginative, restive under advice, impatient under criticism, he lacked caution as a leader and accuracy as a guide. Though fearless as a party chieftain, he fought mostly for compromise, and though ambitious for the Presidency, he desired it for national rather than personal ends. A statesman and not a politician, he hated selfishness in office and greed in public trust, so that his integrity as a man and citizen is free from spot or stain. A gentleman always, he could face down all assaults upon his honor or his name, and if he had not been consumed by the one laudable ambition to be President of the republic, his story would have been one of success, of leadership, of popularity, and of a fame undimmed by the shadow of failure or the cloud of personal ambition. But his record is still that of a great American, and his country will gratefully remember his services, while for years his home here in beautiful Lexington will be a point of pilgrimage for the patriot, the citizen, the American."

THE CLAY MONUMENT.
As seen from Ashland Lawn, across the city of Lexington

AN OLD-TIME CHRISTMAS IN KENTUCKY.

Jack's Discomfiture—Beautiful Kentucky—The Dark and Bloody Ground —Louisville Hospitality—Glimpses of Jackson—At the Hermitage— Old Alfred's Reminiscences—Relics and Stories—The Home and Character of Old Hickory.

S Jack registered for his party at the hotel in Nashville — Jack always assumed this duty, and Uncle Tom declared that it was done with such an air of proprietorship that he always felt his own insignificance — he said to the clerk, as he buried the pen-point in the box of shot:

"Whereabouts does the trolley start, for the Hermitage?. Near here?"

"The Hermitage!" exclaimed the hotel clerk, with the hotel clerk's superior though affable smile; "why, there 's no trolley to the Hermitage. That 's twelve miles off."

"Is that so!" said Jack. "Well, that 's the first time we 've been so far from a lemon. Everything, everywhere, from Norfolk on, has been just a trolley-ride away. What 's the matter with the Hermitage?"

"Oh, that 's all right," the clerk replied, with a twinkle; "but you see, Old Hickory did n't think of trolleys when he settled there. Like to move it for you, sir, but, you see, we can't. It 's a pleasant trip down there, though. Better take it in."

"Why, that 's what we 're here for," said Jack, turning away to join the others, marshaled under Uncle Tom's lead at the elevator.

To them, Jack reported. In the midst of the laugh at Jack's expense that followed, Uncle Tom assured his nephew that his inquiry was entirely unnecessary, as all such details had been duly attended to, and that they would leave for the Hermitage on the morning train.

"Meantime," he said, "we 'll still be loyal to your trolley program,

Jack, and ride out this afternoon to see the Vanderbilt University and the big exposition buildings at the farther end of the city."

They did so, and were amply repaid for the trip, surprised and pleased at the bigness and beauty of Nashville — the great exposition buildings set in a broad, green park ; the State Capitol, with its Grecian outlines, set high on a hill ; and, close beside it, the grave of President Polk, and the fine equestrian statue of General Andrew Jackson, whose home, called by him "the Hermitage," they were now en route to see.

JACK ALWAYS REGISTERED.

Their journey west and south from Lexington had been a delightful one. The boys and girls all fell in love with Kentucky. The green stretch of "blue-grass" country between Lexington and Louisville was a veritable garden-land, and Roger declared that he should prevail on his father to sell out in Boston and buy one of the beautiful estates in Pewee Valley, or some other fair stretch of Kentucky country, and go into the horse business.

At this there was a general shout. The idea of the Boston boy "weakening on his beloved Hub," as Jack expressed it, was too much for them.

"All the same," said Bert, "there's no discount on this, " and he swept his hand toward the verdant landscape that lay on each side of the rumbling train. "That man in the smoking compartment yesterday told us that Kentucky was the Lord's own country ; and it does look like it — on the surface."

"And yet," Uncle Tom declared, "no region in our land has been more torn by ferocity and feud. Think of it! This was 'the dark and bloody ground '— this peaceful-looking landscape!"

"Forest land, though ; not pasture then, I guess," put in practical Bert.

"Of course, much of it ; but just as beautiful then as now, Bert," said Uncle Tom. "But it was the red-man's battle-ground. Here, again and again, Northern and Southern Indians met in fierce struggle for the possession of these choice hunting-grounds ; here hunters and pioneers struggled with the red owners for a foothold. Just a few miles to the south of where we are

"A VERITABLE GARDEN-LAND."

now the Kentucky river winds its way through the region made famous by Daniel Boone; and at our very next stop — Frankfort, the capital of the State —the great frontiersman lies buried in the only six feet of Kentucky soil that, after all he did for this region, he could call his own. There, too, in that same Frankfort cemetery, rises the monument to one whose name and work you must recall — O'Hara, the soldier-poet."

"What, the one who wrote the 'Bivouac of the Dead'?" cried Roger.

"Why, that's the poem that is cut up and posted about among all those soldiers' graves at Arlington," said Jack.

"Oh, yes; just across the river from Washington," said Marian; "I remember that. And the man who wrote that splendid poem is buried here, you say?"

"Just beyond us here, in Frankfort cemetery," replied Uncle Tom, while Christine, looking through the window toward the town they were nearing, repeated softly :

> "On Fame's eternal camping-ground
> Their silent tents are spread,
> And Glory guards with solemn round
> The Bivouac of the Dead."

"Somehow, that poem always just goes through me," said Marian. "It makes me tingle."

"A fine piece of verse," said Uncle Tom. "One stanza not used in Arlington is local, and applies especially to the Kentucky soldiers of 1812 and 1846 who rest beneath their marble monument yonder in Frankfort cemetery:

> "Sons of the dark and bloody ground,
> Ye must not slumber there
> Where stranger steps and tongues resound
> Along the heedless air;
> Your own proud land's heroic soil
> Should be your fitter grave;
> She claims from war its richest spoil—
> The ashes of the brave."

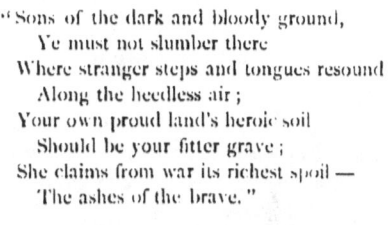

"THE MAN IN THE SMOKING COMPARTMENT."

Just then the train drew into Frankfort, and Uncle Tom pointed out the old and new capitol buildings and told them of Kentucky's contributions to the republic.

"'Your own proud land's heroic soil' has a notable record," he said. "A Kentucky man drew my attention to it yesterday as we wandered about Lexington. Let me see if I can recall it. Two Presidents of the United States— Zachary Taylor and Abraham Lincoln — were Kentucky born, you know, and the one Confederate President, Jefferson Davis. Besides these, two Vice-Presidents of the United States and two acting Vice-Presidents, two Secretaries of State, four Secretaries of the Treasury, three Secretaries of War, one Secretary of the Navy, one Secretary of the Interior, six Postmasters-General, six Attorneys-General, seven Judges of the Supreme Court, two Presidents of the Senate, and six Speakers of the House. That's quite a list, is n't it?"

"I should say so," said Bert.

"Anything left for Ohio?" queried Jack.

"You don't think that Kentucky man's 'Kentucky-ness' made him swell things, do you?" asked Roger.

"Well, his loyalty may have led him into over-appropriation," said Uncle Tom; "for he included James G. Blaine, because the famous Speaker taught school and married his wife in Kentucky, and I suspect one or two

others may have been Kentuckian by his adoption.
Still, it's a strong list, and one not easily paralleled.
Kentucky's a great State, you see."

So they all concluded before they were through
with it. Their two days in Louisville were crowded
with pleasure. The situation, extent, energy, and
stateliness of the city impressed them, its wide
streets and verdant lawns gave to it breadth and
beauty, while its hospitality was avoided only by a
vigorous effort.

But Uncle Tom, with a stern sense of duty,
dragged his "brood" away from the delightful Third-
street mansion where lived a charming Kentucky
woman whom some of the boys and girls had met at
their Maine summer resort by the sea, and who insisted upon keeping them all and indefinitely. So
at last they escaped across the Kentucky border
"by the skin of their teeth," Bert biblically declared,
and reached the southernmost point in their trip
— Nashville and the home of Andrew Jackson.

SOLDIERS' MONUMENT AND TOMB OF O'HARA, FRANKFORT, KY.

The morning after their arrival in Nashville they took an early train on the Lebanon Branch road, running east from Nashville, and, as they made the hour's run through a green and fertile country of rolling land that, so Bert declared, looked "real New Englandy," Uncle Tom gave his young auditors brief glimpses of the remarkable man whose homestead they were approaching.

"A stirring life, from the word 'go,' was that of Andrew Jackson," he said. "We see him first a rough, red-haired, freckle-faced, fatherless boy of the 'piney woods' section of Carolina, picking up a poor living and a poorer schooling. A bluff and boisterous boy, I imagine; something of a bully, but never a coward. Brought up on the border, he was a belligerent before he was in his teens, fighting the British as a boy guerrilla, seeing his brothers and mother die through British cruelty, and early learning the lesson of hatred to the foes of America that clung to him through all his eventful life.

"We next see him a Western emigrant, crossing the border into Tennessee in 1788, when he was twenty-one years old, settling as a lawyer in the new town of Nashville, and taking long horseback rides from courthouse to court-house through a region swarming with Indians and wild beasts — enemies he was obliged again and again to face in fight.

"After this come success, recognition, popularity, advancement. He helps draft the constitution of the new State of Tennessee, is sent to the nation's capital, first as a representative, then as a senator; he becomes Judge Jackson of Tennessee, then General Jackson, finally President Jackson.

"We see him building on his big plantation, toward which we are traveling, a house of logs in 1804. I will show you that very log house, yet standing. There he and his dearly loved wife live for fifteen long years, when, in 1819, he builds the house now famous as the Hermitage.

"We might, if we had time, follow him step by step throughout his steady progress from a 'piney-woods boy' to President. It would be a course checkered with much hard fighting, many personal quarrels, lawsuits, duels, bitterness, and anger, for Andrew Jackson loved hard and hated hard; but there would be in it, too, honesty, integrity, business ability, firmness, courage, loyalty, and love. These were the things that sent him ahead, that gave him popularity, that made people believe in and follow him. Let me give you these steps upward, in just so many words: farmer-boy, soldier-boy, saddler's apprentice, law-student, horse-trainer, lawyer, frontiersman, prosecuting attorney, land speculator, constitution-maker, representative, senator, judge, storekeeper, farmer, flatboat-builder, wholesale shipper, cotton-planter, stock-raiser, militia officer, volunteer soldier, general, conqueror in

ANDREW JACKSON.

the war of 1812, victor in Florida, governor of Florida, United States senator, presidential candidate, President, hero by popular acclaim! — there is a
record of steady progress filling a life of seventy-eight busy years, and punc-
tuated with all those fiery incidents that made Andrew Jackson at once a
terror and a triumph.   I think there is no other figure in American history
whose success is so meteoric, or whose career was so dramatic as that of this
tall, thin, sinewy, strong-faced, stiff-haired, seventh President of the United
States, whom men still love to refer to as ' Old Hickory.' "
    The train, soon after, left them on the platform of the little wayside sta-
tion called Hermitage — a depot, a cross-roads country store, a house or

two in sight, and, stretching all about, green and wooded slopes and pastures.
The girl at the store stepped to the door and shouted, " Jack ! You Jack!" with
such startling earnestness that our Jack really felt uncomfortable.   The other
Jack came, and with him the carriages Uncle Tom had ordered.   Then followed a delightful two miles' drive to where, turning from the pike, they drove
through a shaded roadway up to the doorway of a low, rambling, square-built,
porticoed, two-story house, standing far back from the road — the Hermitage.
      "How perfectly delightful!" exclaimed Marian, as she surveyed the
breezy, hospitable-looking place, which seemed to speak a welcome in every
line and corner of its unpretentious amplitude.

They paid a lingering visit to the
homestead which, with twenty-five acres
of surrounding land, is now owned
by the State of Tennessee, and cared
for by the Ladies' Hermitage Association.   Under the guidance of old Alfred, the last of the Jackson slaves, they
inspected the few, the very few, remaining Jackson relics (for most of them,
unfortunately, have been scattered or
transferred), the house, the grounds,
the garden, and the monument.
      The old fellow proved entertaining,
and a loyal adherent of the " ole gin'ral "
and of " Missus Jackson."
      " Why, I held the ole gin'ral's arm
jest like *dat* 'fore he died," he assured
Roger, grasping the boy's arm ; and he
delighted the girls by holding forth on
" Missus Jackson's " goodness and im-
partiality.
      "She was a good missus," he declared,
" 'n mighty good to the pore folks. She
could sing, and ride a horse as well as
the gin'ral hisself, and she was 'tentive
to her pra'rs and minded her Bible.
Many 's de time," he added reflectively,
" dat Missus has put me, Marse Andrew, and the Injun boy, one after
t' other, 'crost her knee and jest whopped us for bein' owdashus."
      Uncle Tom hastened to explain that " Marse Andrew " was Mrs. Jackson's

THE HERMITAGE—HOME OF ANDREW JACKSON.

nephew and the general's adopted son, while the "Injun boy" was that little Indian orphan, whose story is familiar, who was picked up by Jackson on a Creek battlefield, sent to the Hermitage, and cared for by the conqueror of his race.

"The Hermitage was a great place for children, white and black," Uncle Tom declared. "Andrew Jackson had no sons or daughters of his own, but he loved all children, and there were many nephews and nieces to play about these grounds, while the boys and girls through the country that were named 'Andrew' or 'Rachel' by his admirers were legion."

They wandered through the big breezy rooms of the old-fashioned mansion while Alfred drew their attention to things that seemed to him important — the paper on the halls and stairway, imported from France by Jackson, and put on the walls under his supervision — a monstrous pattern of commingled history and mythology, as impossible in scene as in perspective.

He took them to the wide-porticoed piazzas, up-stairs and down, and showed them just where Jackson stood when he made his last public speech, and he drew their attention to the cedar-shaded walk that led from the gate-entrance. The great cedars that lined it were planted by the "ole gin'ral," so he explained, "in the form of a git-thar."

"A what?" inquired puzzled Marian; and it required a repetition and an explanatory sweep of the hand to show that the old custodian meant that the cedar walk was shaped like a guitar.

Alfred also explained, as he led them about the house to show its proportions, that when the Hermitage was built in 1819 it was just a square blockhouse with a small porch. "But in 1835," he informed them, "the ole gin'ral, 'ca'se he was President, you see, put on dese yere exaggerations," and he indicated the ample pillared porticoes which project from the house at front and rear.

THE OLD HERMITAGE STILL STANDING.
Built 1804.   The smaller building is old Alfred's birthplace.

The children smothered a laugh at the old man's apt though innocent appellation, and then followed him afield to the first Hermitage — the old house of logs, a gunshot away from the later mansion. That, they learned, was Jackson's home at the time of the war of 1812 — the war that made him famous, when, behind the cotton bales of New Orleans (only Bert assured them that there were no cotton bales there at the time of the battle), he forced back the veterans of Wellington and closed a leaderless war with a brilliant victory.

They roamed all about the place, resting again and again in the shade of the great encompassing trees. Then old Alfred grew interested in the enthusiastic young people and made an exception in their case. For he unlocked the gate in the iron fence that encircled the monument and let the boys and girls stand within the temple-like mausoleum that marks the grave of a statesman.

"As simple as Webster's, so far as inscription goes, is n't it?" said Bert. "But it tells the story, just as Webster's did. All the world knows Andrew Jackson."

The girls read twice, carefully, the touching tribute to his wife Rachel that Jackson caused to be carved upon the slab that lies close beside his own.

"Is n't it beautiful?" said Christine. "I don't see, Uncle Tom, how a man who could say such lovely things about his wife could be such a fighter in war and politics."

"Jackson's respect for women was almost knightly in its courtesy," Uncle Tom declared.

JACKSON'S TOMB.

"His affection for his wife was peculiarly deep and strong, and when she died, just before his inauguration as President, he went to Washington, in the midst of shouts of welcome and congratulation, a lonely and broken-hearted man."

"Yes, sir, dat 's de troof," old Alfred affirmed. "I 'member, jest 'fore he

IN OLD TENNESSEE DAYS.

went, de ole gin'ral he planted dese yere willows hisself, beside ole Missus'
grave. Dey was jest switches den, but dey done growed, 'cept dat ar one
what was struck by lightnin'. De ole gin'ral loved dis place. W'en he gits
into his kerridge fer to go to Washington he done tuk off his hat to de house,
jest like it was a lady, and den he dribe away."

It was all very interesting. Yonder, at the old house in the fields, so
Uncle Tom told them, Aaron Burr had been a frequent visitor, and from it

Jackson went to war and victory; here, in the "new" house, Jackson had received Lafayette as a guest, and behind the mansion were spread the long tables for the great barbecue in honor of the famous Frenchman. Here he received the news of his election; here he outlined the action that made his name a power in American politics; here "all the world" came to see and honor him; and here, on a June day, he died, an old man of seventy-eight. The young people felt, indeed, that the Hermitage had been well worth the visit. It seemed, so Christine declared, to put them nearer to the real man with a good and tender side, whom they had only known by the unyielding nickname of "Old Hickory."

A lunch at the Hermitage, a visit to the Confederate Soldiers' Home on the adjoining grounds, a talk with numerous friendly and grizzled old veterans who had worn the gray, a delightful drive back to the station through woodlands vocal with finch-songs and robin-notes, and through the mingling green and white of Tennessee's spring foliage and blossoms, completed this most satisfactory trip to the home of Jackson.

In the fields beyond the country store they waited for the up-train to Nashville, and while they did so, Uncle Tom, as they all sat in the shade of the great hickory-trees, sought to give them a brief summing up of the character of the master of the Hermitage.

"I have already told you," he said, "that I can name no more unique or picturesque figure in American history than Andrew Jackson."

"How picturesque, Uncle Tom?" demanded Bert, who was always very particular as to adjectives. "Can you apply that to such a bluff and gruff old fellow as Jackson?"

The girls remembered the inscription on his wife's tablet, and were inclined to protest against calling him bluff and gruff. But Uncle Tom did not seem to find the boy's words objectionable, and simply assured Bert that anything that occupied a unique or "decorative" position in material or intellectual conditions could be called picturesque.

"Certainly," he added, "nothing could be more noticeably picturesque in character or story than this brave and fiery old fighting-man. No man was ever more devotedly followed, none was ever more cordially hated. Partizans rallied around him as about a tribal chief; enemies raged against him as against the bitterest foe. He came into our political history as a free-lance; his nomination and election upset all the old traditions. The aristocrats prophesied anarchy; the people hailed his inauguration as bringing in the reign of the people. All the starch and show that had held sway in presidential etiquette from Washington's time were overthrown. It was a new departure, and Jackson's election to the Presidency," Uncle Tom declared, " was the most important event in American history from Washington's day to that of Lincoln."

" Jackson was the first ' people's President,' " he said. " More than Jefferson, he was the father of national democracy ; more than Clay, he was intensely, even belligerently, American ; more than Webster, he had what we call, ' the courage of his convictions,' and would live up to what he esteemed right, no matter who opposed it. Absolutely fearless, vigorous in methods, quick in action, emphatic in speech, if he thought a thing should be done, he did it, careless of consequence.

" Not a great man in the sense that Washington and Lincoln were great, he was yet so brave, so outspoken, so determined, and so resolute that he

JACKSON SQUARE AND THE CATHEDRAL, NEW ORLEANS.

silenced all opposition and triumphed over all enemies, while his stern and inflexible honesty rose almost to greatness."

" He did n't go much on civil-service reform, Uncle Tom, did he ? " asked Roger.

" Was n't he the man who said, ' To the victor belong the spoils' ? " Jack inquired.

" No ; he was not the originator of that detestable saying," Uncle Tom replied; "but he acted up to it, for it was the advice of one of his partizans. Even in that, though, was Jackson's picturesqueness displayed. He was intensely loyal to his friends; he was equally vindictive to his foes, and from his administration certainly dates the system of political rewards and punishments which for half a century marred and cheapened American politics and patriotism. Jackson, you see, was the soldier in office. He knew no master save his own will, which, he declared, was the will of the people. And it did appear to be so, too; for the majority of the people believed so thoroughly in him that his two terms as President were at once the most popular the most dramatic and the most effective of those of all the Presidents of the United States up to his time."

RACHEL, WIFE OF ANDREW JACKSON.
In a locket worn by the President.

"He won the battle of New Orleans, and he said 'the Union must and shall be preserved.' I know that much about him," said Jack. "What else?"

"I can't enumerate here in detail, Jack," Uncle Tom replied; but this I can tell you, Andrew Jackson was a patriotic President."

ONE OF "OLD HICKORY'S" SPORTS.—IN A TENNESSEE HUNTING-FIELD.

"No monkeying with the Constitution allowed — keep off the grass — that kind of President, was n't he, Uncle Tom?" said Jack.

"That 's about it — in your peculiar and vigorous speech," Uncle Tom admitted. "With the sternness of the despot he crushed the rebellious attempts of the 'nullifiers,' and saved the Union from disruption; with an equally heavy hand he demolished the institution called the United States Bank, which he considered a menace to the republic; he brought England to terms; made France pay a just but delayed indebtedness; settled disputes of long standing with Denmark and with Spain; and forced Europe to recognize and admit the strength and vigor of America as a nation."

"That 's the talk!" exclaimed Jack, with enthusiasm. "He had some 'sand' about him, General Jackson did."

"He was certainly what we call to-day American and aggressive," Uncle Tom declared. "But he was so from inclination and conviction, not from policy. He was a true man, whatever he did.

"Warm-hearted, fearless, patriotic, honest, and sincere, he lived, the people's idol; and dying, was canonized by all America as the synonym of leadership, force, and mastery.

"He was impulsive, he was hot-headed, he was obstinate. He made many mistakes, and yet even these proved successes; for, in all the history of the republic, Jackson was the only living President who retired from office more popular than when he went in.

"Throughout all this region he was loyally loved. All over the land men were his faithful partizans long after his public life closed, and his last years at the Hermitage were those of a sage and an oracle, to whom men looked for advice and direction. A remarkable man every way, boys and girls, was Andrew Jackson. From the time when, as a plucky boy of thirteen, he refused to clean the boots of the British officer, to the day when he died yonder, at the Hermitage, an old and honored man, his story is well worthy of study, and, whenever studied, will be found suggestive, picturesque, dramatic, American.

"There! I 've talked till train-time. All aboard for Nashville, and good-by to the Hermitage!"

They whirled away toward Nashville. But in the intervals of "Jackson talk" and delight at the Tennessee landscape Jack waxed eloquent over an account of the splendid "coon hunt" that "the other Jack," had told him of, as the Northern and the Southern boy had sat together beneath one of the great shade trees at the Hermitage.

THE LAST PORTRAIT OF ANDREW JACKSON.
Painted at the Hermitage in 1845.

CHAPTER XI

BESIDE THE MISSISSIPPI

Uncle Tom's Latest — Mammoth Cave Explorers — The Birthplace of Lincoln — Across the Prairies — By the "Father of Waters"— Where Grant got His Experience — A Leader's Life — A Hero's Death.

IT was a good three hours' run through regions where the names had a certain familiar sound to those who had studied the campaigns of the Civil War — Nashville and Franklin and Bowling Green. Suddenly Uncle Tom started to his feet.

"Come, boys; gather up your traps," he said. "Put on your hats, girlies. The next station is ours."

"The next station?" exclaimed Marian, who for the time was immersed in the new "St. Nicholas," which Uncle Tom had bought for her at Nashville. "The next, did you say? Why, we can't be back again at Louisville as soon as this!"

"A hundred miles from there, my dear," laughed Uncle Tom. "This is just a little joke of mine. Here we are — Glasgow Junction! All out for Mammoth Cave!"

"Mammoth Cave! No, Uncle Tom! Are we really going there?" came the surprised and exultant chorus. "Oh, isn't that just splendid!" And a demonstration of affection was made upon this scheming uncle who had worked upon them another of his delightful surprises.

In the midst of it all the train stopped, and soon after they were lunching at the comfortable little railroad inn; and, before long, the short branch railway bore them into the honeycombed hill region and up to the rambling hotel of logs which stands in its pleasant woodsy park, upon the crust of earth so wondrously seamed and tunneled by the crossways and caverns of the mighty Mammoth Cave.

Will they ever forget that delightful burrowing in the ground — the descent from the upper world; the barred iron gate at the great black mouth of the cavern; their "convict garb of blue jeans," as Jack described it; the swinging torchlights; the jolly party of young folks — students from a Bowling Green institute — with whom they made the trip; the endless pas-

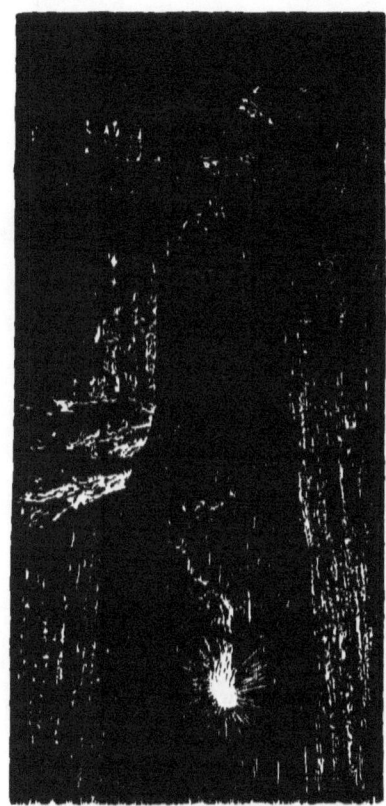

sages "stretching from nothing to no-where," as Marian expressed it; the great domed chambers; the yawning pits, the fantastic forms and figures formed by stalactites and stalagmites; the giant's coffin; the bridal altar; the star chamber; the elephant's head; the corkscrew; the statue of Martha Wash-ington; the memorial cairns, or monu-ments, piled up by generations of vis-itors; the flaring fires lighted by the guides to bring out strange formations or gruesome contrasts? These, and all the other surprises, delights, wonders, and what Christine called "shivery sensations" of that eight-mile walk un-derground, will stand out among the chief memories of their "famous-men hunt," because the experience was at once so unexpected and so novel. And next morning, as they sped northward toward Louisville, the personally con-ducted five held a mass meeting in their parlor-car compartment, and returned a special vote of thanks to Uncle Tom, duly engrossed in a shaky, "railroady" hand on a telegraph blank, and as shakily signed by each one of them.

THE BOTTOMLESS PIT, MAMMOTH CAVE.

But when they had left the curious cave region behind them, and were speeding Louisville-ward again, Uncle Tom led their minds back to the tem-porarily deserted channel of historic Americans, and advised them that they were passing over storied ground.

" Up and down these highways," he said, "contending armies moved in the fierce days of the Civil War, struggling for the possession of Kentucky, a border State.   Off there to the east, at Perryville, was fought the most des-perate battle ever waged on Kentucky soil.   It was brother against brother, and Kentucky was saved to the Union.   But even more than by the valor of

HODGEN'S MILL AND DAM ON NOLIN'S CREEK.
Three miles from Lincoln's birthplace; town of Hodgensville in the background.

the boys in blue was Kentucky saved to the Union by the wisdom and patience and will of Abraham Lincoln, himself a Kentucky boy."

"That's so," said Bert; "he was born in Kentucky, was n't he? And so was Jefferson Davis, too."

"Yes; some miles southwest of us, in Todd County. From this region, by the way, came also Mrs. Lincoln, whose name was Mary Todd. Strange, is n't it, how lines of coincidence cross?" Uncle Tom answered. "But, as I was saying, I esteem the saving of Kentucky by Abraham Lincoln one of his chief claims to greatness. It was a triumph of sound judgment and inexhaustible patience. No other man—not Clay himself, the great pacificator —could have achieved the beneficent ends aimed at and attained here in Kentucky by Lincoln, the great emancipator, whose early home lies not far away from the very region we are now traversing."

"Oh, are we so near his birthplace?" cried Roger. "Whereabouts is it?"

Uncle Tom consulted a moment with the porter, crossed to the window, and then said:

" Now, look—look out of the window—here, on the left. See that little stream coming down through the pastures? Now we are crossing it. Boys and girls, this is Nolin's Creek ; and on the banks of this little stream, twelve miles farther up, Abraham Lincoln was born."

At once the boys' hats were doffed in salute to this, the most important river in Christendom, so enthusiastic Jack declared, and the girls fluttered their handkerchiefs toward it: for, as you know, this peripatetic five had been schooled in Uncle Tom's belief that Abraham Lincoln was the world's greatest man.

Even as they rumbled over the bridge and looked across country toward the rolling land where, when all was forest or scarcely-won clearing, the great American was born, Uncle Tom dropped into poetry, as he sometimes would, and gave to his boys and girls those fine lines from Lowell's matchless tribute in his " Commemoration Ode."

" It seems to fit just in this place," he said:

> " Nature, they say, doth dote,
>   And cannot make a man
>   Save on some worn-out plan,
>   Repeating as by rote ;
> For *him*, the Old-World moulds aside she threw,
>   And, choosing sweet clay from the breast
>   Of the unexhausted West,
> With stuff untainted shaped a hero new,
> Wise, steadfast in the strength of God, and true."

" How was he different from anybody else?" asked Bert. " You call him 'new' and ' the American.' Have n't we had other men as American? What 's the matter with Franklin ? "

" Nothing is the matter with him, Bert," said Uncle Tom. " Franklin, in a way, was the most characteristic American ; certainly, up to the time of

"ALL ABOARD FOR ST. LOUIS!"